"Ouch, my ears!" Haley cried. "Tori, are you going to open the door, or what?"

Tori hesitated. The girl looked harmless enough, but Tori knew her mother didn't like her to let strangers into the house.

"Who is it?" Tori called out.

"It's Veronica Fouchard," the girl responded. She brought one blue eye close to the peephole, trying to peer back at Tori.

"Who's Veronica Fouchard?" Haley asked.

"I have no idea," Tori answered.

The girl began to bang loudly on the door. "Are you going to let me in? Or do I have to stand out here all night? Hello! Tori!"

Surprised to hear her own name, Tori pulled open the door. "How do you know who I am?" she asked.

Veronica tossed her hair. "I'm amazed you don't know who *I* am." Veronica was dressed in a long black coat and black high-heeled boots. Two matching large red suede suitcases stood by her feet.

"I should know you?" Tori asked.

"Of *course*," Veronica responded. She fixed her blue eyes directly on Tori's. Her mouth twisted into a little smirk. "Imagine, not knowing your own *sister*!"

Super Edition #2

WEDDING
SECRETS

Melissa Lowell

Created by Parachute Press, Inc.

A SKYLARK BOOK

NEW YORK • TORONTO • LONDON • SYDNEY • AUCKLAND

The author gratefully wishes to acknowledge B. B. Calhoun for her help in writing this manuscript.

With special thanks to Darlene Parent, director of Sky Rink Skating School, New York City

RL 5.2, 009–012

WEDDING SECRETS

A Skylark Book / January 1997

Skylark Books is a registered trademark of Bantam Books, a division of Bantam Doubleday Dell Publishing Group, Inc. Registered in U.S. Patent and Trademark Office and elsewhere.

Silver Blades® is a registered trademark of Parachute Press, Inc.

The logos of the United States Figure Skating Association ("USFSA") are the property of USFSA and used hereon by permission of USFSA. All other rights reserved by USFSA. USFSA assumes no responsibility for the contents of this book.

ISBN 0-553-48523-7

Published simultaneously in the United States and Canada

Bantam Books are published by Bantam Books, a division of Bantam Doubleday Dell Publishing Group, Inc. Its trademark, consisting of the words "Bantam Books" and the portrayal of a rooster, is Registered in the U.S. Patent and Trademark Office and in other countries. Marca Registrada. Bantam Books, 1540 Broadway, New York, New York 10036.

PRINTED IN THE UNITED STATES OF AMERICA

OPM   0 9 8 7 6 5 4 3 2 1

Super Edition #2

1. Tori

Tori Carsen smiled at her reflection in the mirror.

"Oh, Tori, that blue velvet is beautiful on you." Martina Nemo sighed. "You're lucky to have so many great clothes."

"I know," Tori replied.

It was late Thursday afternoon. Tori and Martina were in the locker room of the Seneca Hills Ice Arena. They had just finished skating practice. As members of Silver Blades, one of the country's top ice-skating clubs, Tori, Martina, and their friends practiced skating twice a day, every day. Sunday was their one day off.

Tori didn't mind practicing hard. She was determined to be one of the best female singles skaters ever. But then, Tori liked to be the best in whatever she did. She even liked to be better-dressed than everyone.

"This is one of my mom's designs," Tori told Martina, twirling to show off the velvet dress.

"It's perfect for you," Martina said. "Just the right color for your blond hair and blue eyes."

Tori's mother, Corinne Carsen, ran her own clothing design company. She made all of Tori's skating outfits, and sometimes she designed clothes for special occasions—such as the blue velvet Tori wore now.

"The best part is that it's one of a kind," Tori confided. "I'm the only one in the world who has this dress."

Tori's other skating friends gathered around her.

"I'd be happy with a velvet dress that *wasn't* one of a kind," Martina joked. Martina came from a large family and didn't often get to buy fancy new dresses.

Haley Arthur pulled an oversized sweatshirt over her T-shirt and bright orange leggings. "I don't know, Tori," Haley teased. "Isn't a velvet dress pretty fancy for school?" Haley's brown eyes twinkled under her red bangs. She was a tomboy and never dressed up. She was also a talented pairs skater and Tori's best friend.

"You didn't *really* wear that dress to school today, did you?" Nikki Simon asked. She glanced at Tori in surprise. Nikki also skated pairs. She had wavy brown hair and green eyes.

"Of *course* not." Tori turned to Haley and frowned.

"Only *you* wouldn't notice what your best friend was wearing all day long." Tori held out the skirt of the dress. "I changed because tonight is a really special occasion."

"Really? Where are you going?" Haley asked.

"Out to dinner at the Circle View restaurant," Tori answered. "Roger's coming, too."

"Roger Arnold? Your mom's fiancé?" Nikki asked. Mrs. Carsen and Roger Arnold were engaged to be married.

Tori nodded. "My mom said they have something to tell me—a big surprise. I hope it's about redecorating my room," she added. "My mom knows how much I want my room done over."

"You're so lucky," Amber Armstrong commented.

Amber was the youngest member of their group of friends. She was only eleven. But she was also one of the most talented singles skaters in Silver Blades. Some people thought Amber was even better than Tori. Tori didn't agree.

"Well, you know my mom," Tori replied. "She likes to do stuff for me. She really cares about me."

Nikki nudged Martina and smiled. Mrs. Carsen's "caring" was famous around the ice rink. She often came to practice with Tori, to watch—and to criticize. Mrs. Carsen complained that Tori didn't work hard enough. Tori usually complained that her mother embarrassed her. Still, they were very close.

"You know, my mom even picked out the song for my new routine," Tori said. "It's called 'Forever.'"

Tori slipped her coat on. "I'd better hurry. Later, you guys! I can't wait to find out about the big surprise."

Mrs. Carsen's silver Jaguar pulled up in front of the Circle Tower Hotel. An attendant opened Tori's door. Tori slid out and followed her mother inside. Mrs. Carsen removed her white cashmere coat and draped it over her arm, revealing the elegant gray dress she wore underneath. She patted her ice blond hair and lifted her chin. If there was one thing Mrs. Carsen knew how to do, it was make an entrance. "First impressions last a lifetime," Tori's mother often said. *"They're* what people always remember."

Tori removed her own jacket and smoothed the skirt of her dress. Her mother smiled approvingly. Together, they crossed the lobby toward the glass elevators by the fountain on the far side of the room.

Roger Arnold was waiting for them by the fountain. "The two loveliest women in Seneca Hills!" he cried. He took Mrs. Carsen's hands, and she leaned forward for a kiss.

Tori stared at the fountain for a moment. She always felt a little embarrassed when her mom and Roger acted lovey-dovey.

Roger led them both toward the bank of elevators. He turned to Tori. "That's a pretty dress. Did your mother design it?"

"Yes," Tori answered proudly.

"Corinne, you have so much talent," Roger told Mrs. Carsen. "No wonder your boutiques are doing well at the stores." Roger owned Arnold's, the chain of department stores. Several of his stores had sections in them called Corinne Carsen Boutiques, where they sold Tori's mother's designs.

"I've been thinking that your boutiques might go over well in the California stores." Roger paused. "Of course, not right away. It will have to wait until after—" He caught himself and stopped.

Tori's mother glanced at him quickly. "Yes, of course."

Tori eyed them both. "What are you talking about? After *what*? Does it have to do with the surprise?"

Her mother laughed. "You'll hear all about it soon enough."

The elevator arrived, and they rode up to the restaurant on the top floor of the hotel. A few moments later they were seated at a table beside a large plate-glass window. A candle flickered in the center of the table. Seneca Hills lay spread out below them under a star-filled sky.

"I'm glad we have a table near the window," Tori said.

"I wanted everything to be perfect," Roger responded. Tori watched as he reached across the table and took her mom's hand. They sure are doing a lot of romantic stuff tonight, she thought.

The waiter arrived with the menus. "We'll have lobster and champagne," Roger ordered. "And sparkling apple cider for the young lady," he added.

"Champagne? Why are you getting that?" Tori asked. "I thought champagne was only for really special occasions, like New Year's Eve."

"Not always." Roger grinned.

Tori stared at him. She was used to eating in fancy restaurants such as the Circle View. But she knew that champagne and lobster were *extra*-fancy foods.

The drinks arrived, and Roger cleared his throat. "I'd like to make a toast." He raised his glass. "To the most beautiful bride Seneca Hills will ever see."

Tori's mother smiled. "Thank you, Roger. I only hope I can pull it all together in time."

"Pull what together?" Tori demanded, setting down her glass. "Is this about the surprise? Tell me!"

Her mom turned to Tori. "Sweetheart, Roger and I have made a big decision. We're going to get married right away."

Tori stared at her mother in surprise. "You mean *tonight*?"

Roger laughed. "Oh, no, not that soon. I couldn't deny your mother the pleasure of planning a big, fancy wedding."

Tori's mother laughed, too. "The pleasure *and* the trouble." She turned to Tori. "Roger and I compared our business schedules. We realized that if we don't get married now, we'll have to wait another year and a half."

"And we don't want to wait that long," Roger added.

"I guess," Tori mumbled. She frowned. It had taken her a while to get used to the idea of having a new stepfather. She wasn't sure she felt ready for the actual wedding. "How soon will it be?" she asked.

"Next month, on February twenty-third." Mrs. Carsen sighed. "It won't be easy, pulling together a large, formal wedding so quickly. There are a million things to think about. Food, flowers, music, invitations—"

"Can I invite my friends?" Tori asked.

"Sure," Roger responded. "We want you to have fun."

"We'll probably invite over two hundred people," Mrs. Carsen said. "Naturally, I want everything to be absolutely perfect. Including the design for my wedding gown. I'm going to need your help, Tori. With everything."

Tori was getting excited. Planning a party for two hundred people, including Tori's friends . . . this could be great!

"Of course I'll help, Mom," Tori said.

Her mother beamed at her. "I knew I could count on you. This is a very important occasion for me. For all of us." Her mother took Tori's hand and gave it a squeeze. "You and I have always been there for each other, sweetheart. The Carsen team, right?"

Tori nodded. For as long as she could remember, they had been a team. Tori's father had left them when Tori was only a baby. Her mother was the only parent Tori had ever really had.

"Tori, I want you to be a special part of the wedding," Mrs. Carsen continued. "I want you to be my maid of honor."

"Really?" Tori's eyes grew wide. Maid of honor—it sounded so important. Tori pictured herself standing up beside her mother in front of the crowd of people. "Do I get to wear a gown, too?"

"Of course. I'll design a formal dress for you." Her mother squinted, momentarily lost in thought. "How about something with a high neck? In pale blue, I think. Or should I use pink? You look beautiful in pink."

"Pink sounds nice," Tori agreed. "But how about a scoop neck? They look better on me."

"We'll decide later," Mrs. Carsen said. "But, you know, this is a good opportunity for me to showcase some formal-wear designs. The newspapers are bound to cover the wedding. The better we both look, the better it is for business."

"We might get our pictures in the paper?" Tori leaned forward eagerly. This was sounding more and more exciting!

"You're the expert, Corinne," Roger told her. "You and Tori just go ahead and plan it."

"Don't worry, we will," Tori responded happily.

She couldn't wait! An extra-special new dress, a huge, fancy party, and her picture in the paper. There might even be an article about the wedding. After all, her mom was one of the most glamorous people in Seneca Hills. And Tori was her only daughter—and her maid of honor!

Tori sighed happily. "This wedding is going to be the best thing that ever happened to me!"

2. Haley

At a large, formal wedding, the bride usually has several attendants. Everyone wants to be a bridesmaid! However, the bride must be gracious—and use humor—in limiting the number of attendants she will choose.

—The Complete Wedding Book

Haley rushed into the locker room. She dropped her backpack and her skate bag on the floor. She had just had an idea about how to end her star-lift with a special flourish, to really make the pose match the feeling of her new music. She could hardly wait to try it out.

The locker room was empty. Haley pulled off her black parka and threw it on a bench. She kicked off her boots, sending them flying. She tugged off her sweater, easing it over her head so that it wouldn't snag the silver earring in her left ear. She tossed the sweater over another bench.

The locker room door swung open, and Amber hurried in. Amber often arrived early for practice.

"Hey, Haley," Amber called. She set her skate bag

down by her locker and looked around for a place to sit. The benches were covered with clothing.

"Who else is here?" Amber asked.

"Nobody," Haley answered.

"All this stuff is yours?" Amber gaped at the mess in disbelief.

Haley followed her gaze and laughed. "I guess it is hard to believe. I'll clean up before everyone else gets here." She stood up and began gathering her things together.

"Speaking of everyone else," Amber began, "how's Tori doing with her triple toe loop?"

Haley raised an eyebrow. She liked to stay out of the rivalry between the two skaters. Before she could answer, Tori rushed into the locker room. She was wearing her powder blue parka and a new pink scarf. The glow of her cheeks was almost as bright as the scarf.

"Haley—I am so glad you're here!" Tori clutched Haley's arm. "I wanted to call you last night, but we got home really late. Wait till you hear!"

"Hear what? What's going on?" Amber asked.

"Oh, hi, Amber," Tori said. "You might as well listen, too. The news will be all over town soon."

"What news?" Haley asked.

Tori took a deep breath. "Mom and Roger have decided to get married right away."

"Hey, that's great," Haley said. "I guess your mom is really excited."

"Yeah, and they're having a *huge* wedding," Tori bubbled on. "With a band and tons of flowers and hundreds of guests. And I get to be the maid of honor!" Tori raised her chin in the air.

"Wow! That sounds really important," Amber said.

"It is," Tori assured her. "My mom's designing a special dress just for me. Long and very formal. The reception will be the biggest thing Seneca Hills has ever seen. Everybody who's *anybody* is going to be there."

"Everybody, huh? Sounds pretty crowded," Haley joked.

"And I can invite some of my friends, too," Tori added. Her blue eyes sparkled with excitement.

"That's fantastic! When is it?" Amber asked.

"February twenty-third," Tori answered.

"February? But that's next month," Haley pointed out. "I thought you said they'd decided to get married right away."

"Next month *is* right away when it comes to a formal wedding," Tori stated. "My mom has a book called *The Complete Wedding Book*. It says it could take a whole *year* to organize something like this."

"A *year*? To plan a party?" Haley said. "That's nuts."

Tori rolled her eyes. "Not a party, Haley, a formal wedding. But it will be so much fun planning everything!"

"Sounds like a real pain to me," Haley said.

"What's a pain?" Nikki pushed open the locker room door. Martina followed.

"Making plans—for Tori's mother's wedding," Haley announced. "Her mom's decided to get married next month."

"And Tori gets to be the maid of honor," Amber told her.

"Tori, that's great," Nikki said.

"I love weddings," Martina added. "My cousin Christina got married last year. I wore a beautiful yellow dress."

"Maybe you could wear it to this. Tori's friends are invited, too," Amber added.

"Well, I don't know how many friends I can ask. My mom and I have to make out the guest list," Tori said.

"What about Roger? Does the groom get to invite anyone?" Haley teased.

Tori sighed. "Of course. But a wedding is really about the *bride*, Haley—and her maid of honor, of course. *The Complete Wedding Book* says the groom doesn't have a big part in the planning."

"Sounds to me like the groom has the *best* part," Haley commented. "If I ever get married, I hope my husband will let *me* be the groom."

Everybody laughed. Martina checked her watch. "Wow, we'd better get out on the ice, you guys."

Haley hurried out of the locker room with the others. Her skating partner, Patrick McGuire, waved to her. He was already finished with his warm-up.

Patrick was fifteen, two years older than Haley, and a sophomore in high school. Like Haley, he had red hair and brown eyes. People often said they looked like brother and sister.

"Late again, Haley," Patrick called.

Haley removed her skate guards and glided up to him. "I'll warm up extra fast," she answered. "Anyway, it's Tori's fault that I'm late. She was talking so much about her big news."

"What big news?" Patrick asked.

"Her mom's getting married next month. You won't believe what a big deal they're making out of the whole thing." Haley shook her head in disgust.

"Oh, you girls *love* this wedding stuff," Patrick teased.

"Not me!" Haley shot back. "Anyway, let me warm up. I want to show you an idea I had for our star-lift. It really fits the music." Their music was the popular, upbeat song "We're a Team."

Haley quickly warmed up and took her position on the ice next to Patrick. They started out with side-by-side crossovers to build up speed. Then they each performed a quick double flip, side by side. Haley did a scratch spin and gestured to Patrick, who followed with a scratch spin of his own. Next they both did four Arabian cartwheels, one right after the other, and quickly jumped into side-by-side flying camels.

Next came the star-lift. Patrick reached for Haley's hands. He spun her around in a tight turn, then reached for her hip and lifted her. At the top of the lift, Haley held her position, opening her arms wide. A few moments later Patrick eased her back toward the ice.

Haley landed perfectly, then pulled Patrick toward her. "Put your arm around my waist," she said. Patrick held her with his right arm, and Haley did a backward layover.

"Great idea." Patrick beamed at her. "Like the song says, we're a lean, mean team!"

Haley giggled. "It doesn't really say that—but you're right. We are," she told him. "Let's try it again."

They worked on the lift at afternoon practice, too. It was coming along great. Finally it was time to leave. Haley changed out of her skating clothes and headed for Kathy's office. Kathy, the coach, usually gave Haley a ride home, since Haley's mom worked late.

The door to Kathy's office was closed, and Haley realized that Kathy must be having a meeting. She headed back to the rink and flopped down on one of the bleachers. A moment later Tori sat down beside her.

"Tori! What are you still doing here?" Haley asked in surprise.

"My mom's supposed to pick me up, but she had a business meeting first," Tori explained. "I guess she'll be here in a minute." She paused. "Haley, I'm really worried about something. I kept thinking about it all through practice."

Haley turned to her friend in concern. "What is it? What's wrong? A problem with one of your jumps?"

"No, it's about the wedding," Tori said. "I'm worried that my mom won't have any bridesmaids."

"But I thought *you* were the bridesmaid," Haley said.

"No, I'm the maid of honor," Tori corrected her. *"The Complete Wedding Book* says the bride in a formal wedding needs bridesmaids, too."

"So then your mom will get some," Haley said.

Tori shook her head sadly. "No, we already talked about it. Usually the bridesmaids are the bride's closest friends or her sisters. But my mom doesn't have any sisters. And most of the women she knows aren't close friends. They're people she met through her business."

"It seems like a lot of silly rules," Haley said. "Doesn't that crazy wedding book say you can change the rules?"

"No way. And this wedding has to be *perfect*!" Tori exclaimed. "Don't you see?"

"I *don't* see," Haley admitted. "What's the big deal about bridesmaids, anyway? I mean, they don't actually *do* anything, do they?"

"They're very important! They march down the aisle ahead of the maid of honor and the bride," Tori explained. She sighed. "If I were getting married, I'd just ask everyone from Silver Blades to be my bridesmaids."

"So why don't you get *your* friends to do it? I

mean, it's just walking down the aisle, right?" Haley laughed. "I think they could handle that. Even me."

Tori gaped at her. Then she broke into a wide smile. "Haley, that's a fantastic idea! You guys can be bridesmaids!" She stopped. "I wonder what *The Complete Wedding Book* would say. I mean, you're not exactly my mom's *friends*."

"But we all know her really well," Haley pointed out. "We see her at practice just about every day of our lives."

"That's true," Tori said. She grinned. "It would be so much fun. We could have you, and Jill, of course—"

"Jill?" Haley cut her off. Jill Wong was a close friend from Seneca Hills. But she had left Silver Blades to train at the prestigious International Ice Academy in Denver. "Jill's in Colorado."

"So?" Tori said. "She can fly back for the wedding."

Haley shot her an incredulous look. "You expect Jill to fly all the way back here just to walk down the aisle at a wedding?"

"Sure," Tori said. "It's a big honor. Besides, a bridesmaid does more than just walk down the aisle."

Haley frowned. "How much more?" she asked.

"Well, there's this special way you have to walk. I'll show you—the book tells all about it," Tori said with authority. "And I think you're part of the receiving line afterward."

"The receiving line?" Haley echoed. "What's *that*?" She didn't like the sound of it at all.

Tori was still chattering away. "I wonder if you guys should wear pink, like me. Or maybe the bridesmaids' dresses should be different, so that my dress stands out more." She gave Haley a little squeeze. "Oh, Haley, this is such a great idea."

"Yeah," Haley said halfheartedly. "Great."

"There's my mom!" Tori leaped up and waved across the rink. "I'll tell her your idea on the way home. Call you later, Haley!"

"Okay," Haley answered as Tori hurried away. She made her way back to Kathy's office. The door opened, and Roger Arnold stepped out.

"Hey, Mr. Arnold!" Haley greeted him. "If you're looking for Tori and Mrs. Carsen, they just walked out the door," she told him. "You could catch them if you hurry."

Roger glanced around quickly. "Okay, thanks," he answered. He turned toward the exit. But Haley noticed that he didn't seem to be hurrying at all. In fact, he seemed to be dragging his feet.

Not that I blame him, Haley thought. If I were Roger, I'd probably want to stay as far away from Tori and her mom as possible—at least until this whole wedding thing is over.

And if I were smart, that's what *I* would have done, Haley realized. Now I'm going to be a bridesmaid. I'll have to wear some prissy pink dress and learn some silly way to walk! And follow a bunch of stupid rules I don't even understand.

If only she could take back her whole idea. But she knew Tori better than that. Once Tori liked an idea, there was no stopping her. And Tori obviously *loved* this idea.

Face it, Haley told herself. You can't get out of this now. Someday you've got to learn *not* to open your great big mouth!

3. Tori

The bride must be ready to face any and all challenges—everything from last-minute changes in the menu to Uncle Walter's sudden demand to be seated away from Cousin Hildegard! It is wise to expect the unexpected.

—The Complete Wedding Book

Tori leaned toward her mother. "It's totally beautiful, Mom," she blurted out. They sat together on the white couch in the Carsens' living room. Mrs. Carsen balanced a large sketchpad on her lap. A drawing of a spectacular wedding gown took up one whole page. The gown had full sleeves that narrowed to points at the wrists. The floor-length skirt also narrowed to the ankles. An elegant train swept behind the dress.

"Are you sure?" Mrs. Carsen frowned at the drawing. "I'm not happy with the neck. Is it too square? Maybe I should give it more of a V neck."

"I think a V neck. Definitely." Tori glanced across the room. "Don't you think so, Haley?"

Haley was spending the night. At that moment she was sprawled on the carpet, reading one of Tori's skating magazines.

"Haley," Tori tried again, "don't you think a V neck would be nice for my mom's wedding gown?"

Haley raised her eyes. "Sure, a neck sounds fine."

Tori groaned. "You're so pitiful! How can you sit with your nose in a magazine at a time like this?"

"Leave her be," Mrs. Carsen told Tori. "The neckline doesn't matter when I'm still stuck on the color." She shook her head. "I saw a lovely pale yellow at one of my fabric supplier's, but I don't see myself in yellow."

"How about pink, like my dress?" Tori suggested.

"Well, we couldn't wear *exactly* the same color. But the right shade of pink might work," Mrs. Carsen said. "I know! Petal pink, a shade so light it's almost off-white."

"That sounds really pretty," Tori agreed.

"Petal pink might be just the thing." Mrs. Carsen twirled a pencil. "It would be nice with your pink dress, and then we could do the bridesmaids' dresses in the same family of colors but in a darker shade—maybe maroon or burgundy."

"Perfect," Tori declared. She was thrilled that her mom liked the idea of letting her friends be bridesmaids. She was also glad that her mother planned to make their dresses different from Tori's dress. Tori would still be wearing a one-of-a-kind design.

"We'll have to do a *deep* maroon," Tori's mother went on. "If it's too bright, we could have a problem with Haley's red hair."

Haley glanced up with an alarmed expression on

her face. "What's that? You want me to change my *hair color* for this?"

Tori laughed and tossed a throw pillow at her. "No, silly. We're talking about the color of your dress. Pay attention."

Mrs. Carsen checked her watch. "Oh, my goodness, Roger will be here to pick me up for dinner soon! I'd better get ready." She stood up and smoothed down her black slacks.

Tori spotted the open sketchpad on the couch and picked it up. "Mom, you don't want to leave this out where Roger can see it, do you?"

"Oh, of course not." Mrs. Carsen tucked the sketchbook under her arm. "Thanks, Tori. I'm afraid I have a lot on my mind lately." She hurried out of the room.

"What was wrong with leaving the sketchbook out?" Haley asked.

"Don't you know?" Tori stared at her. "The groom isn't supposed to see the wedding dress until the wedding. It's really bad luck."

"It is?" Haley asked. "Why?"

"I don't know why," Tori said in frustration. "It just *is*, that's all. Everybody knows that."

"Well, I think it's crazy," Haley said. "Who made up these rules, anyway?" She grinned. "Wait, I bet I know—the grooms."

"The *grooms*?" Tori asked. "Don't be silly. Why would they make up something like that?"

"So they wouldn't have to listen to the brides and

the maids of honor plan every single little detail of the wedding dress," Haley finished.

Tori laughed.

Later that evening Haley and Tori lay on the rug in front of the television, watching *Night of the Killer Lizards*.

"Ugh." Tori made a face. The film's heroine, a girl with long, dark hair, screamed just before her head was bitten off by a giant lizard. Tori glanced at Haley, whose eyes were glued to the screen. "Hey, want to call Jill in Colorado? I tried her yesterday, but she wasn't at her dorm. I still have to tell her about the wedding and about being a bridesmaid and every-thing—"

"Later," Haley cut her off. "The movie's almost over, okay?"

"Okay." Tori gazed around the room. She spotted *The Complete Wedding Book* on the coffee table. She opened it and admired the photos of bridal gowns, flowers, and wedding cakes.

A few minutes later Haley switched off the televi-sion. "That was great."

"Mmm." Tori studied a photo of bridesmaids in pale blue dresses. They held bouquets of delicate white roses.

"I wonder what kind of flowers we should carry," Tori mused. "Maybe something pink, to match my dress."

Haley groaned. "Don't start on that wedding stuff again. You act like *you're* the one getting married."

"Well, I *am* the maid of honor," Tori pointed out. "*And* the daughter of the bride. I'm practically as important as the bride is, you know."

Tori closed her eyes. She could see it all. She would float down the aisle in her beautiful long pink dress. Her friends, dressed in their maroon bridesmaids' gowns, would wait for her at the end of the aisle. Everyone's eyes would be on Tori as she smiled prettily. Cameras would flash on either side of her.

"This is going to be one of the biggest days of my life," Tori said. "And I—" She was interrupted by the chimes of the doorbell. "Who could that be?"

Haley shrugged. "Your mom and Roger?"

Tori shook her head. "My mom would use her key."

Haley stood up. "Only one way to find out."

"Wait," Tori said, following her. "We have to check through the peephole first." Tori's mother always warned Tori to be careful about answering the door when she was home alone.

Tori squinted through the peephole. On the other side of the door she spotted an unfamiliar face. It belonged to a girl about her own age or a little older. The girl had large blue eyes with dark lashes and auburn hair cut just below her chin. Her hair was parted on the side so that it fell slightly in front of one eye, and a black beret was perched on her head. Whoever she was, she was amazing-looking.

Haley elbowed Tori. "Who is it?"

"I don't know," Tori whispered, her eye still at the peephole. "Some girl."

At that moment the girl reached out impatiently and pressed the doorbell again. The chimes rang out behind Haley's head.

"Ouch, my ears!" Haley cried. "Tori, are you going to open it, or what?"

Tori hesitated. The girl looked harmless enough, but Tori knew her mother didn't like her to let strangers into the house.

"Who is it?" Tori called out.

"It's Veronica Fouchard," the girl responded. She brought one blue eye close to the peephole, trying to peer back at Tori.

"Who's Veronica Fouchard?" Haley asked.

"I have no idea," Tori answered.

The girl began to bang loudly on the door. "Are you going to let me in, or do I have to stand out here all night? Hello! Tori!"

Surprised to hear her own name, Tori pulled open the door. "How do you know who I am?" she asked.

Veronica tossed her hair. "I'm amazed you don't know who *I* am." Veronica was dressed in a long black coat and black high-heeled boots. Two matching large red suede suitcases stood by her feet.

"I should know you?" Tori asked.

"Of *course*," Veronica responded. She fixed her blue eyes directly on Tori's. Her mouth twisted into a little smirk. "Imagine, not knowing your own *sister*!"

4. Tori

It is desirable to include as many friends and relations as possible in the wedding plans. But distant relations need not be included in the more important wedding roles.

—The Complete Wedding Book

"**M**y *what*?" Tori exclaimed. "Is that a joke?"

"Tori doesn't have a sister," Haley added.

Veronica swept into the entryway and unbuttoned her coat. "Well, we're not *exactly* sisters. But close enough. Where are Roger and Corinne?"

"Out to dinner," Tori answered.

Veronica slipped out of her coat and handed it to Tori. Tori slung it across the marble table in the entryway. She tried not to stare at Veronica's outfit—but it was spectacular.

Veronica wore a green suit the color of seafoam. The miniskirt ended in a slight flare, with a narrow black band around the hem. The fitted jacket was trimmed with black triangular buttons. Veronica carried a matching black triangular purse. Tori thought

Veronica looked incredible. But she wasn't about to say so.

"How could you be my sister?" Tori demanded. "How do you even know us?"

"Well, I don't know Corinne. Not yet. But I'm sure we'll get along. Roger has excellent taste in women. After all, he married Adele—my mother."

"Mr. Arnold is married to *your* mother?" Haley's eyes widened in shock. "But he's supposed to marry *Tori's* mother!"

"Wait a minute. I know who you are." Tori stared at Veronica. "I remember now. I once heard that Roger was married before. But not for very long. And I remember that the woman he married already had a daughter, from her first marriage. That's you, isn't it?" Tori demanded. "You're not my sister. You're Roger's stepdaughter!"

"*Ex*-stepdaughter, if you want to get technical." Veronica fixed her eyes on Tori. "But you can't *really* be Tori."

"Of course I'm Tori," Tori snapped.

"I thought Tori was fourteen." Veronica examined Tori from head to toe. "You look about eleven. But I guess American girls take longer to grow up." She nodded at her coat, which was lying across the table. "That really needs to be put on a hanger, you know. It's impossible to get creases out of that fabric." She gazed around and then headed into the living room.

Tori left the coat where it was. She and Haley followed Veronica into the living room. "So what are you doing here, anyway?" Tori asked.

"I came for a visit." Veronica sat on the couch and removed a lipstick from her purse.

"A visit? Now?" Tori laughed. "This isn't a great time for visitors, you know. We're planning a wedding. A big wedding," she added.

Veronica raised her eyebrows. "Of course I know that. After all, Roger *is* practically my family. And Corinne will be family, too, after they get married." She paused. "You shouldn't leave my bags out on the doorstep, Tori. It might rain, and they *are* suede, you know."

Tori gaped at her. "Who do you think you are, ordering people around? If you think I'm going out there to get your bags, you can just—"

"*I'll* get them," Haley cut her off.

"Thank you," Veronica told Haley.

Tori glared at Veronica. "Does my mother know you're here?"

"Well, I *told* Roger to tell her," Veronica said.

"Well, I guess he didn't," Tori retorted. "I'm sure she would have told me if she knew you were coming."

Veronica shrugged. "Actually, I went to Roger's first. The doorman told me he was out and gave me this address." Veronica blotted her lips with a tissue. She gazed around, then dropped the smeared tissue into a crystal ashtray.

Tori glared at her again.

"Too bad I missed them," Veronica continued. "I'm sure they would have wanted to take me to dinner."

"They wanted to be alone," Tori replied. "Or they would have taken *me* with them."

Veronica shrugged. Haley returned with the suitcases. "These bags are so cool," she said, admiring the bright red suede.

"I picked them up in Switzerland," Veronica told her. "I went to school there once. Switzerland has the best schools, you know. My mother and I have lived all over Europe—most recently in Italy and Spain. We live in France now."

"Wow." Haley was obviously impressed. "Can you speak all those languages?"

"French and Italian are my best," Veronica said. "My Spanish is so-so."

"Wow," Haley said again. "Tori and I speak only English."

"That's all we *need* to speak in Seneca Hills," Tori pointed out.

"Our friend Jill knows some Chinese, though," Haley went on. "Her family is Chinese American."

"That reminds me, we have to call Jill right now," Tori said.

"We can call her later." Haley turned to Veronica. "Say something in Italian."

"What do you want me to say?" asked Veronica.

"Um, I don't care, whatever you want," said Haley.

"Haley," Tori urged. "Come *on,* we have to call Jill. We have to tell her she's going to be in the wedding." Tori raised her chin and turned to Veronica. "My friends are going to be bridesmaids at the wedding, you know. I'm the maid of honor."

"Non mi importa, facciamo come vuoi tu," Veronica replied.

"What does that mean?" Tori asked.

"It means 'I don't care, whatever you want,'" Veronica answered.

"What?" Tori blinked in surprise.

"It's what your friend asked me to say in Italian." Veronica smirked.

"Oh, I get it," Haley said, laughing. "That's pretty funny."

There was a click as the front door opened. "Hello, we're home," Tori's mother called.

"Mom!" Tori cried in relief.

Mrs. Carsen strode through the doorway into the living room. Roger was beside her. "Veronica?" he exclaimed, spotting her on the couch.

"Oh, my goodness!" Mrs. Carsen blinked in surprise. "We weren't expecting you until—never mind," she finished.

Tori gaped at her mother. "You mean you *knew* she was coming? And you didn't tell me?"

"We weren't sure," Mrs. Carsen began.

"But this is a terrible time for company!" Tori protested.

Veronica ignored her. She extended her hand toward Tori's mother. "It's a pleasure to meet you, Corinne."

"It's a pleasure to meet you, too, dear," Mrs. Carsen responded.

"Mom," Tori objected, "why didn't you tell me that she—"

Her mother glanced at her. "We'll talk more about this later, Tori."

Roger regarded Veronica. "I can't believe how grown-up you are. Aren't you close to Tori's age?"

"Oh, she looks much older than Tori," Mrs. Carsen replied.

Veronica tossed her hair. "I'm fifteen. I'll be sixteen this summer."

"That's not much older than me," Tori said.

"Well, Veronica just seems older," Mrs. Carsen replied. "I suppose it's from living in Europe. By the way, that's a lovely suit."

"Thank you. My mother's tailor in France made it." Veronica stroked the collar of her jacket. "He makes all our clothes."

"It's beautiful. I suppose you're hungry after your trip, Veronica," Mrs. Carsen said. "Tori, come and help me get some refreshments."

Tori followed her mother out of the living room. As soon as they were alone she turned to her mom. "Why didn't you tell me she was coming?"

"Because I didn't really know," her mother said.

"Roger and I spoke about a visit, but it was supposed to be after the wedding. I'm as surprised to see her here as you are."

"Well, tell her to leave," Tori urged. "Tell her she came at the wrong time."

"Don't be silly, Tori." Mrs. Carsen opened a drawer and slipped out a large silver tray. She grabbed some fruit and cheese from the refrigerator and arranged it on the tray with some crackers. She reached into a cabinet and began placing crystal glasses on the tray. "Now that she's here, we have to make her feel welcome," Mrs. Carsen added.

"Why?" Tori asked.

"Tori, listen to me." Mrs. Carsen frowned. "Try to be extra nice to Veronica. She's in a new place, and, well, things aren't easy for her now. She needs our understanding." She paused as the piano sounded in the living room. "Oh, that must be Veronica playing. How beautiful."

Tori listened to the tinkling notes. "Maybe it's Haley. She took piano lessons when she was little." But even as Tori said it, she knew it couldn't be Haley. It was a classical piece, complicated and fast. Haley could never play anything so hard.

Tori followed her mother back into the living room. Veronica was at the white baby grand piano. Roger and Haley stood nearby, gazing at her in admiration.

Veronica's fingers flew over the piano keys. Her eyes were closed, and her body swayed dramatically to the music. Tori glanced at her mother, who stood absolutely still. The tray was forgotten in her hands as she also closed her eyes.

Veronica finished the piece with a flourish. She glanced around with a smile. What a show-off, Tori thought.

"Veronica, that was *beautiful*!" Tori's mother exclaimed.

"Magnificent," Roger agreed.

"I couldn't do that if I took lessons for a hundred years," Haley added.

"I feel like I *have* been taking lessons that long," Veronica joked.

Roger laughed. "I knew Veronica began studying piano when she was very young," he explained. "And I'm so glad to see you've kept it up," he told her.

"Absolutely. Feel free to use the piano anytime while you're in town," Tori's mother offered.

"You want her to practice *here*?" Tori asked.

"Why not?" her mother asked. "Roger doesn't even have a piano at his apartment. In fact, Roger doesn't have much at all in that apartment." Mrs. Carsen was thoughtful for a moment. "Veronica," she suddenly said, "how would you like to stay here with us?"

"Oh, no, I couldn't, really," Veronica answered politely.

"Why not? They have a guest room right across the hall from Tori's room," Haley told her.

"Haley's right," Mrs. Carsen said. "In any case, we have more room than Roger has in that bachelor apartment. It's settled. Veronica will take the guest room."

"Well, thank you very much," Veronica told her.

"My pleasure," Mrs. Carsen replied. "I think it's wonderful that you're here. You and Tori will be great friends. And it will be so nice for Roger to have you at the wedding."

"At the wedding?" Tori stared at her mother. "She's going to be at the wedding?"

"Of course," Tori's mother answered. "In fact, I have a lovely idea. Veronica, we've asked two of Tori's friends to be bridesmaids in the wedding. Why don't you join them?"

"Mom! No!" Tori gasped. "We don't even know her!"

Veronica glanced briefly at Tori out of the corner of her eye. She turned to Mrs. Carsen. "*Merci!* I mean, thank you very much, Corinne. I'd *love* to be in the wedding." Veronica smiled sweetly up at her. "I feel like family already."

Tori's eyes narrowed. Well, you're *not* my family, she thought. And you never will be. Not if I can help it!

5. Jill

The first important wedding decision is choosing the date. Then begins the countdown. The members of the wedding party, as well as the guests, will be as excited as the bride and groom as they wait for the magical day.

—The Complete Wedding Book

"**Y**ou're ready, Jill," Ludmila Petrova announced. "I will schedule you to take the senior-level test in the next few weeks."

"Do you mean it?" Jill Wong clapped her hands in delight.

"I mean it," her coach said.

"Thank you, Ludmila!" Jill exclaimed. She hesitated. "Should I keep practicing now?"

"Yes. You have a few minutes of ice time left. And there is no substitute for practice," Ludmila told her. She gave Jill a rare smile. "Show me the end of your routine one more time."

Jill nodded and glided to the center of the ice rink. She raised her arms high over her head.

The senior levels! Jill was thrilled. And nervous. Jill knew she was a very talented skater—one of the top

singles skaters in the country. Talented enough to
have been asked to train at the International Ice
Academy in Denver. The Academy was one of the
country's best skating schools. And Ludmila was one
of the best—and toughest—coaches.

Jill had worked long and hard at her skating, first
with Silver Blades and then at the Academy. She had
done well in competitions. But so far she had skated
at the junior level. Taking the senior-level test was the
next goal in her career. A very important goal.

If Jill passed the test, she'd qualify to skate in the
most important competitions in figure skating. It was
what every skater dreamed of.

"Begin, Jill!" Ludmila called to her.

Jill took a deep breath and launched into the end-
ing of her routine. She easily landed the most difficult
jump—a triple flip–triple toe loop combination. Then
she flew through the rest of the program, which
ended with a beautiful sit spin. Jill held the pose,
knowing she had skated flawlessly. She felt as if she
might explode with pride and happiness.

Ludmila nodded briskly. "That's fine, Jill. See you
tomorrow."

Jill nodded back. Coming from Ludmila, the few
words were high praise. Jill quickly changed out of
her practice clothes and hurried across campus to
Aspen House, her dorm. Everywhere she looked, the
ground was covered in snow. The trees glimmered in
the sunshine. Jill thought it was extra beautiful that
day.

She bounded down the pathway, moving so fast that she didn't see Jesse Barrow heading directly toward her.

"Watch out!" Jesse called as Jill almost bumped into him.

"Oh, Jesse! Hi. Sorry," Jill answered sheepishly.

Jesse grinned. He shook his smooth blond bangs off his forehead. His gray eyes twinkled. "You sure seem happy today."

"I *am* happy!" Jill felt herself blush a little. Jesse was fifteen. He was one of the Academy's best male singles skaters. Plus he was cute and sweet. And he always went out of his way to talk to her. Jill realized that he was interested in her, but she already had a boyfriend—Ryan McKensey. She had promised to be loyal to Ryan, even while she was in Denver.

Ryan lived in Seneca Hills. He had just turned sixteen. Ryan had dark hair and warm brown eyes. He was quiet and thoughtful. Ryan had seen Jill through some tough times, including the time she had broken her foot and had to drop out of the Academy for a while.

"Jesse, Ludmila wants me to take the senior-level test," Jill answered. "Really soon, too!"

Jesse's eyes sparkled even more. "Wow, that's great, Jill. Congratulations! You'll be eligible to compete in Skate U.S.A."

"Oh, that's right!" Jill gasped. "I was so excited, I didn't even think of that." Skate U.S.A. was open only to competitors in the senior division. It was a nationwide competition, attracting the top skaters in the country. Jill wasn't eligible for the event as a junior skater. But she could compete as a senior skater.

"I'll do it!" Jill burst out. "I'll compete. That is, *if* I pass the test," she added.

Jesse regarded her. "You will. You have all the moves. If you just believe in yourself, you'll do fine."

"Thanks, Jesse. That's good advice." Being with other serious skaters such as Jesse was one reason Jill loved studying at the Academy.

"Hey—let's celebrate your big news," Jesse suggested. "I'll buy you a soda in the snack bar."

Jill hesitated. Ryan wouldn't be happy about her going out with another guy. "Thanks, but I can't. Uh, I've got lots of homework," she fibbed.

"Okay, sure." Jesse looked disappointed. "Catch you later."

Jill waved to Jesse and sped up the hill to her dorm. She hurried into her room. Her roommate, Bronya Comaneau, was practicing pliés, a ballet move like deep knee bends.

Bronya was from Romania. She had short light brown hair, held back now with a wide headband. She wore an old black leotard. Bronya rested one hand on the back of her desk chair for balance as she worked out.

"Hi, Jill!" Bronya called. She counted out in Romanian: *"Unu, doi, trea, patru."*

Bronya did ballet exercises every day. Most Academy students did weight training and stretches as

well as their daily skating practice. But Bronya had
begun ballet training back in Romania. Her former
coach thought ballet helped skaters add form and expression to the more athletic moves. Bronya agreed.

"How was practice?" Bronya asked.

"Great," Jill replied. "Ludmila said she wants me
to take the senior-level test. I don't know when," Jill
added in a quieter voice. After all, she didn't want to
sound like a show-off. She knew that Bronya could
hardly wait to compete at the senior level herself.

"You are so lucky." Bronya suddenly smiled.
"Sorry. I shouldn't have said 'lucky.' You worked
hard for this, Jill. But I admit it—I wish I were in
your place."

"Oh, Bronya." Jill glanced into her roommate's big
brown eyes. "You'll take the test soon. I know it.
You're ready, too."

"Yes," Bronya said in a low voice. There was a
knock on the door. "Come in!" Bronya called.

Amanda Parrish, a younger girl who lived on Jill's
floor, poked her head in the door. "There's a phone
call for Jill."

"Thanks." Jill hurried down the hall. She hoped it
was her parents. She couldn't wait to tell them her
good news.

Or maybe it's Ryan, she thought. She grabbed the
phone. "Hello?"

"Jill, *finally*!" a familiar voice replied. "You are *so*
hard to reach, do you know that?"

"Tori!" Jill couldn't help feeling a bit disappointed.

Ryan hadn't called yet this week, and she was a little worried about it. "Hi. What's up?"

"Oh, Jill, so much has happened! I don't know where to start," Tori said in a rush. "My mom's getting married—next month, on February twenty-third. They decided not to wait any longer."

"Actually, I have some news, too—" Jill began.

Tori cut her off. "*And* I'm helping her plan the whole wedding! Hundreds of people are coming. Mom says it will probably be in the newspaper."

"Wow!" Jill was impressed. "That sounds pretty exciting."

"Plus I'm going to be the maid of honor," Tori added. "But guess what else? Guess who the bridesmaids are? Haley—and *you!*"

"Me?" Jill repeated. "But I'm not even *in* Seneca Hills."

"So? You can come back," Tori told her. "Oh, Jill, it's going to be so much fun. My mom's designing me a gorgeous long pink dress. And you and Haley are going to wear long maroon dresses."

"Haley's wearing a dress?" Jill asked. She could barely believe it.

"Of *course*," Tori replied. "She can't wait. Oh, but I've got some bad news, too."

"What is it?" Jill asked with concern.

"Ugh. This awful girl named Veronica," Tori answered. "She's Roger's ex-stepdaughter, from when he was married before. She's his ex-wife's daughter—it's complicated. Anyway, she lives in Europe, so

Roger hasn't seen her in a long time. But she showed up here last night. And now she's staying with us!"

"Really?" Jill was curious. "What's she like?"

"Horrible! A total show-off," Tori said. "She wears these unbelievable clothes that some tailor makes especially for her. And she's always playing the piano and speaking French and bragging. I can't stand her!"

Jill smiled to herself. In a way, Veronica sounded a lot like Tori. After all, Tori's clothes were all specially made for her by her mother. And Tori could be a show-off sometimes.

"How long is she staying?" Jill asked.

"Too long! That's the worst part," Tori wailed. "Veronica's going to be here for the wedding. And my mother invited her to be a bridesmaid!"

"Well, I guess Veronica *is* sort of like a relative," Jill pointed out.

"She's not related to *anyone*!" Tori insisted.

"I guess. Actually—" Jill hesitated. Going back to Seneca Hills meant buying a plane ticket. That could be a big problem.

Jill's family was large and didn't have a lot of money. Training as a skater was expensive. There were lessons to pay for, rink time, costumes, and skates, not to mention room and board at the Academy.

The Wong family had sacrificed so much for Jill's skating. Plus she had just flown back home for Christmas. How could she ask her parents to buy her another ticket so soon, just to go to Tori's mother's wedding? And what about paying for the bridesmaid's dress? Any dress that Mrs. Carsen designed would cost a small fortune. Jill couldn't ask her family to pay for that.

Jill swallowed hard. Tori never had to worry about money. Jill couldn't help feeling embarrassed to mention it to Tori.

"Actually *what*?" Tori demanded. "Don't tell me you think Veronica should be a bridesmaid!"

"No, I didn't say that, Tori," Jill answered. "I'm just not sure I can come all the way from Colorado."

"Jill!" Tori exploded. "You're supposed to be my *friend*!"

"I *am* your friend," Jill objected. "You know that."

"Well, I need you there. I'm not going through this wedding without all my best friends. It's us against Veronica," Tori explained. "Besides, it's going to be the most glamorous event in the history of Seneca Hills. Everyone will want to go. Believe me, you don't want to miss it."

"But Tori, I—" Jill began.

"Good, then it's settled," Tori declared. "Listen, Jill, I have to go. My mom is working on the sketch for my dress, and I want to see how it's going. Talk to you soon.'" Tori hung up the phone before Jill could say another word.

Jill stood with the receiver dangling from one hand. How could she ever make Tori understand how she felt?

6. Tori

A formal wedding is usually followed by a reception, with dinner and dancing. Guests should be treated to a memorable celebration, for it is the first party the bride and groom will give as a married couple. Therefore, it is the bride's special duty—and pleasure—to make sure that nothing goes wrong with the reception arrangements.

—The Complete Wedding Book

"And the worst thing is sharing a bathroom with her," Tori complained. "I could barely find my toothpaste this morning. Veronica left her junk all over the sink again."

It was time for Friday afternoon practice. Tori and the other members of Silver Blades were changing in the locker room.

"What does she look like?" Amber asked. "How old is she?"

"Fifteen," Haley answered. "But she acts a lot older."

"I'll tell you the way she acts," Tori shot back. *"Annoying."*

The group made their way out into the arena. The

Zamboni was cleaning the ice, so they leaned against the railing to wait.

"I don't see why Veronica had to visit now, just in time for the wedding," Tori continued.

"Why *did* she come now?" Martina asked.

"It does seem weird," Nikki said. "I mean, it's January fifteenth. Shouldn't she be in school?"

"Maybe school's on a different schedule in Europe," Haley suggested.

"Who knows? I just wish she were anywhere but here." Tori sighed. "Veronica acts nice in front of my mother and Roger, but when we're alone, she's really nasty. Like, yesterday she told me my hair was too dry and I should do something about my split ends!"

"Maybe she was trying to be helpful," Martina suggested.

"Was it helpful when she said I had thick ankles?" Tori asked. "Plus she acts like I'm her maid or something."

"Well, I saw Veronica acting bossy," Haley admitted. "But you can act bossy yourself, Tori," she pointed out.

"I do *not* act bossy," Tori protested.

"Still, maybe you should give Veronica more of a chance," Nikki told her. "She is in a strange country and all."

Tori frowned. "Whose side are you guys on, anyway? I—" Tori stopped in surprise. "Hey, look! There she is!"

Tori pointed across the rink as Roger and Veronica

pushed through the main door of the arena. They spotted Tori and headed toward her. Veronica was dressed in a shiny silver parka, black jeans, and black boots. Her black beret was perched on her head, and she wore a pair of silver sunglasses.

"Surprise!" Roger called cheerfully.

Veronica pushed her sunglasses down and peered over them with a bored expression.

"What are you guys doing here?" Tori asked.

"I thought Veronica would like to watch you skate and meet your friends. After all, I'm marrying into a family of skaters. I mean, Veronica and I can't skate, but it's important to you and your mom. We'd both like to know more about that part of your lives," Roger said. He glanced at his watch. "When does practice end today, Tori?"

"Six o'clock," Tori told him. "But you don't have to stay. Mom's picking me up." She glanced at Veronica. "We're supposed to go to the Circle View tonight. Alone."

"Actually, there's been a change of plans," Roger explained. "Corinne decided to head over there early, before the catering office closes. So I *will* pick up you and Veronica. The four of us can have dinner together at the Circle View."

"Oh. I see," Tori said, barely hiding her disappointment.

Roger turned to go. "See you at six," he called.

Haley turned to Veronica. "Hi," she said. "Remember me? I met you at Tori's house the other night."

"Oh, yeah," Veronica said. "Hi."

"That's a really great parka," Haley said. "Is it from Switzerland, too, like your suitcases?"

Veronica fingered the silver fabric. "Actually, it's from Paris. Silver's the rage there this year."

"It's so . . . different," Haley told her. "You can't find cool stuff like that in Seneca Hills."

"Really?" Veronica shrugged. "I could pick one up for you the next time I'm in Paris."

"That would be great!" Haley nudged Tori. "See—she's *nice*," Haley whispered.

"It's an act," Tori whispered back. "Are you going to watch us practice?" she asked Veronica. "Because—"

"Oh, I'm not staying," Veronica answered. She glanced over her shoulder. "Is Roger gone? Good." She began walking toward the exit.

"But—where are you going?" Tori asked.

Veronica laughed. "Did you really think I was going to hang out in this ice-cold rink and watch a bunch of kids ice-skate? I'm going to find some fun in this boring town." She tossed her hair. "See you at six."

Tori stared after her. "How rude!" she cried.

"Wow," Martina said. "She *was* rude."

"You guys just don't know her," Haley protested.

"Neither do you," Tori pointed out.

"Well, I know that she thinks I'm a kid and that our town is boring," Nikki commented.

"Finally, somebody is on *my* side!" Tori said with a grin.

Kathy Bart, one of the Silver Blades coaches, strode quickly toward the group. "All right, people! The Zamboni is gone. You should be working, not gossiping."

"Sorry, Kathy." As Tori hurried with the others toward the ice, she grabbed hold of Nikki's arm. "I'm glad you see how Veronica *really* is," she whispered.

"Yeah. I wonder where she went, anyway," Nikki replied.

"I don't know. But I can't wait to tell my mom how she sneaked off." Tori smiled in triumph. She turned and skated to the far end of the ice, where Dan Trapp, her coach, was waiting for her.

Dan greeted her cheerfully. "Okeydokey," he said. "Let's try something different today. *You* tell *me* how to improve your routine."

"Not another one of your crazy exercises," she complained. Dan was famous around Silver Blades for his method of coaching. He was always telling kids to "get in touch with their feelings" about skating. "Can't I just skate my routine?" Tori asked.

"Sure," Dan responded. "Let's see your stuff, kiddo."

Tori took her position on the ice. She began with a series of spread-eagles, circling the rink.

Her first jump was a double Lutz–double loop combination she'd been doing for almost two years. She landed it easily. Then came the triple toe loop. Tori bent her legs and pushed off. She gained just enough height to complete three revolutions in the air. She landed squarely and launched into a triple salchow–double loop combination.

She ended her routine with another set of spread-eagles and a layback spin. She held her final position for about one second, then skated over to Dan.

"Pretty smooth, huh?" she asked.

Dan shrugged. "Technically, it was good, but—" He paused and raised his eyebrows. "You tell me what it needs."

Tori groaned. "Don't lecture me about *feeling* the music again, please!"

Dan smiled. "Feeling the music is one of the differences between being just a skater and being a real artist. Give it another try, okay, Tori?"

Tori sighed and glanced at her watch. Six o'clock suddenly seemed a very long time away. Somehow she made it through the rest of practice, but she wasn't happy with her routine anymore.

Things didn't improve as she sat in the backseat of Roger's car, listening to Veronica go on and on. Veronica was raving about a trip she had taken.

"Spring is the best time to go," Veronica announced. She smiled at Tori over the back of the seat. "Have you seen the gardens in Rome?"

"You *know* I've never been to Rome," Tori answered.

"I suppose I am pretty lucky. My mother always said that travel was an important part of my education."

"I can't wait to tell *my* mother about some of your latest travels," Tori muttered under her breath. "Like that trip you took away from the rink today."

"What's that, Tori?" Roger asked, craning his neck.

"Oh, nothing." Veronica waved her hand. "Tori's just making a little joke."

"We're here," Roger announced. "But what's this?" He raised his eyebrows in surprise.

Mrs. Carsen was pacing angrily in front of the Circle Tower Hotel. Her cashmere coat was wrapped tightly around her, and her face was red with anger.

"Darling, why didn't you wait for us in the restaurant?" Roger asked her.

"I am *never* going to eat there again!" Tori's mother fumed.

Tori leaned out of the car window. "Mom, is everything okay?"

Mrs. Carsen marched around the car and pulled open the front passenger-side door. "Veronica, let me sit down, please."

"Why, of course, Corinne," Veronica said. She scrambled out of the car and hopped into the back with Tori.

"My car's in the hotel garage," Mrs. Carsen explained. "But I'm too angry to drive. Roger, just get us out of here."

Tori leaned toward the front seat as Roger pulled out of the long driveway. "Mom, what happened? Is it something about the wedding?"

"The Circle Tower is booked for special occasions through *March*!" Tori's mother answered. "We can't have the wedding reception there."

"Oh, Corinne, that's too bad," Roger said.

"It's a disaster!" Mrs. Carsen pressed her hands to her head. "I don't know what to do."

"Isn't there anyplace else?" Veronica asked.

"The Circle View is the best restaurant in Seneca Hills," Tori said. "Nothing else is as good. Mom, are you sure they can't help?"

"I tried everything," her mother responded. "I offered to pay more. I said it would be excellent publicity for them. It was no use. They wouldn't budge."

"I suppose someone else reserved the day," Roger said.

"The restaurant could cancel the other party," Tori's mother replied. "*If* our business was important to them." She glanced out the window. "Roger, where are you taking us?"

"To Burgess," Roger answered, naming a nearby town. "There's a nice café where I eat lunch once in a while. Their food's good. The place isn't big enough for the wedding, but it will do for tonight."

They stopped at a light. Tori noticed Veronica staring out the window. "What's that place over there?" Veronica asked, pointing toward a large building with columns across the front.

Roger glanced out his window. "That's the Whitehall Hotel. It's big, but they don't have a restaurant," he said.

"The Circle View could cater the food!" Veronica said. "Why don't we hold the reception there?"

"We?" Tori repeated. "It's not *your* reception, Veronica."

Mrs. Carsen turned to glance out the window. "That's an excellent idea! It would be almost as good as having the reception at the Circle View."

"Are you serious?" Tori couldn't believe her ears. Planning the reception was supposed to be her job. Hers and her mother's. Not Veronica's.

"It's already late," Mrs. Carsen said. "We'll have to come back tomorrow. I'm going to Tori's practice, but she'll be through early. We can go afterward."

"Sure. You decide, Corinne," Roger said.

Mrs. Carsen twisted in her seat. "Tori, I guess the two of us will go over right after practice. How does that sound?"

Tori brightened. "Sure, Mom," she answered, shooting Veronica a triumphant look.

Finally, she thought. Now things are back on track. It's just Mom and me in charge of the wedding again!

7. Haley

As the wedding day grows nearer, a smart bride will consider handing over some of the prewedding tasks to others. The groom, the maid of honor, or one of the bridesmaids can help out—as long as they are trustworthy and efficient.

—The Complete Wedding Book

It was the following Saturday. Haley waited outside Tori's front door—right on time for her fitting. The door was answered by a man wearing a white jacket. He held a large binder under one arm. "I'm Charles Lee," he said. "In the wonderful world of the Carsen-Arnold wedding, I'm the cake designer. Are you in the wedding, dear? Help me out, we've got a houseful of busy people."

"Uh, I'm a bridesmaid, I guess," Haley answered.

The man's face lit up with a smile. He turned to yell over his shoulder. "We've got another bridesmaid here!"

A young blond woman appeared. She carried a bolt of light pink fabric. "Oh, you want Zophia. She's got them. Come with me."

Haley followed the woman through the living room

toward the stairs. On the way she caught a glimpse of Mrs. Carsen. She held a phone between her shoulder and her ear and was talking while scribbling furiously on a pad of paper. Nearby stood a short, heavy woman with dark hair. The short woman kept trying to show a brochure to Tori's mother, but Mrs. Carsen waved her away.

"Wow!" Haley was amazed at the commotion. "What's going on?"

The blond woman smiled. "Just a Saturday at the bride's house—five weeks before the wedding. I see it all the time. This is actually pretty calm, compared to some weddings. Follow me. The girls are up here."

She led Haley to the upstairs den. Inside, an older woman with red hair stood next to a chair. Tori stood on the chair. The woman wore a pincushion on her wrist and was busy measuring Tori's waist.

"Haley! You made it just in time," Tori said with pleasure. "This is Zophia," she said, introducing the woman with the red hair. "She'll measure you next."

"No hurry," Haley said.

Tori held out a small piece of maroon velvet. "This is the material for the bridesmaids' dresses. Isn't it pretty?"

Haley took the swatch of fabric. "Well, I don't know that much about this stuff, but isn't it kind of *small*?"

"Haley!" Tori rolled her eyes. "It's a sample, not the whole dress! My mom and I love it. We chose it together. We're doing everything together," she boasted. "Well, not *everything*. There's one thing I have to do myself—choose her wedding present."

"She must be hard to shop for," Haley said.

Zophia glanced up. "Oh, you don't need to get your own mother a wedding gift, dear."

"But I *want* to get her something," Tori said. "My mom and I are extra close. And I want whatever I get her to be really special."

The door swung open, and Veronica rushed in. Haley thought she looked very dramatic in a sleek black cashmere tunic buttoned over a white turtleneck. Her auburn hair was pulled back from her face with a wide black band.

"Hey, Veronica," Haley greeted her. "Great outfit."

"Thanks." Veronica glanced at her and turned to Zophia. "I'm ready for my fitting now."

"Actually, *Haley's* next," Tori said. She paused and peered at Veronica. "That's funny, my mother has a tunic just like—hey!" Tori shouted. "That *is* my mother's tunic! Does she know you're wearing that?"

"No. So what? Relax, Tori," Veronica said. "I'm going shopping later, and I didn't have anything else to wear."

"But you can't wear that," Tori told her. "My mother will kill you! It's one of her best, and—" Tori's eyes widened in horror. "What's that stain?" she cried out.

Veronica brushed at a sticky spot on one of the

sleeves. "It's nothing. I spilled some juice, that's all. Your mom can have it cleaned."

"You're crazy," Tori nearly shouted. "Mom's right downstairs, and when she sees you—"

"Your mother's still here?" Veronica finally looked nervous. "I thought she went out! Listen, Tori, don't you *dare* tell her I took this outfit. I'll—"

"You'll take it off, right now," Tori demanded. She stepped down from the chair and took a step toward Veronica.

"Hey, Veronica, you'd better do what she says," Haley told her. She shot Tori an uneasy glance.

Veronica scowled. She unbuttoned the tunic and practically threw it at Tori. "Here—I don't feel like wearing it now, anyway," she said.

Tori lifted the tunic carefully in her arms and studied the stained sleeve. "Look at this mess!"

Zophia took the tunic from her, folded it, and slipped it into her tote bag. "A little club soda will clean it up nicely," Zophia said. "Don't worry, Tori— I'll fix it for you later." She winked. "Mama won't see."

"Oh, thank you, Zophia," Tori said. She glared at Veronica.

Veronica ignored her. "I'm ready now," Veronica told Zophia. She climbed up on the chair.

"It's Haley's turn," Tori told her again.

"That's okay, I'll wait," Haley quickly assured her. She leaned close to Tori. "Don't set Veronica off again."

"Thanks. At least now you see the kind of stunts Veronica pulls," Tori whispered back. She gave Haley a grateful look.

Zophia began working on Veronica's measurements. Veronica stared at a sketch that was lying on a table. The bridesmaids' dresses would be long, with a round neckline and short sleeves.

"The dress is a good style," Veronica said. "But it would be better with a matching evening jacket."

"That's a *terrible* idea," Tori told her. "And you—"

"Now, girls," Zophia interrupted. "Let's try to make nice. You won't fight with your friends at the wedding, will you?"

"What friends will be at the wedding, anyway?" Haley asked, trying to change the subject.

"I don't know. I have only four invitations," Tori admitted. "I thought I'd ask Nikki, Martina, and probably Dani."

Danielle Panati had once been a member of Silver Blades. She had quit skating, but she and Tori were still good friends.

"Aren't you inviting Alex and Patrick?" Haley asked.

"I can't ask one and not the other," Tori replied. "And I have only one more invitation."

Veronica smirked. "If we were in France, I could invite *tons* of cute guys to the wedding," she said. She stepped down from the chair. "If you need me for anything, I'll be in my room." She sailed out, and

Haley climbed onto the chair. Zophia began to take Haley's measurements.

Tori stuck out her tongue at Veronica's back. *"Her* room. Ugh. She acts like she owns the place!" Tori exclaimed.

"I'm sorry about your mom's sweater," Haley told her.

"That's okay," Tori replied. "I guess Zophia will fix it. I just wish my mom could see what Veronica is really like. And I wish we could get Veronica out of the wedding," she added.

"Did you tell your mom how she went off the other day instead of watching us practice?" Haley asked.

"Yeah," Tori replied. "She said that of course Veronica wanted to explore a new place, and that we shouldn't expect her to be interested in skating if she's not a skater!"

"Oh. Well, I guess I see why she said that," Haley said.

Tori shook her head. "Veronica is bad news, Haley. I don't trust her one bit."

"Try not to think about her," Haley suggested. "And try not to be too jealous."

"Jealous?" Tori asked. "What are you talking about?"

"Well, you seem to be a little upset that people are paying attention to Veronica," Haley went on. "You have to admit, she isn't like anyone we know in Seneca Hills."

"No, because people in Seneca Hills are *nice!*" Tori said.

"Come on, Tori, she's not *that* bad. You could try to like her," Haley said. "Who knows? You might even be friends someday."

"I will *never* be friends with her," Tori insisted.

"Now, now, girls. Enough arguing. Think how beautiful you'll all look in your new dresses," Zophia told them with a smile.

Tori slowly smiled back. "Yeah. Oh, Haley, this *is* going to be fun! You, me, and Jill, all in the wedding!"

"Finished," Zophia announced to Haley. She turned to Tori. "Do you think your mother will agree to add the matching evening jackets? If she does, I'll need additional measurements."

"She'll think it's a *terrible* idea," Tori declared. She turned to Haley. "Does Veronica really expect my mother to take her fashion advice?"

Mrs. Carsen stuck her head into the room. She looked exhausted, and her voice was strained. "Zophia, we've got to work on my gown now."

"We're done anyway, Mom," Tori told her.

"Good. But you'll need to take more measurements from the girls later, Zophia," Mrs. Carsen said. "I'm going to add an evening jacket to their dresses."

Tori's mouth dropped open in shock. "You are?"

"Yes," her mother answered in a distracted tone. "Veronica suggested it, and it's a great idea. They're showing those jackets on the fashion runways in Paris now, you know."

"That's fine," Zophia said, glancing at Tori.

"Christine has chosen some fabric samples for the jackets. She's downstairs. Can you look at them? All of you. We can use a few extra pairs of hands." She left the room.

"I can't believe this," Tori complained to Haley on the way downstairs.

Haley shrugged. "It's only a jacket, Tori."

Christine, the young blond woman Haley had seen earlier, was waiting in the living room. She had unwrapped and spread out several bolts of maroon fabric. Zophia, Haley, and Tori helped hold up the materials while Mrs. Carsen studied them.

"These fabrics all look the same to me," Haley remarked.

"Oh, not at all," Christine said. "They're different tones of maroon."

"And we need to compare the way the different fabrics drape and fall," Mrs. Carsen added.

Haley shrugged. Just then the doorbell rang. Mrs. Carsen's face turned white. "It's *Roger*! He's early!"

"Don't let him see! Quick! Hide everything!" Tori cried.

There was a sudden flurry of activity. Everyone scurried around, rewrapping the fabrics and hiding the sketches of the wedding gown.

"Somebody tell him to wait!" Zophia commanded.

"I'll do it," Haley offered. She hurried to the door and peered out the peephole. Roger Arnold waited outside.

"Just a minute, Mr. Arnold," she called through the door.

Roger rang the bell again. "What's going on in there?"

The telephone began to ring, too.

"Haley! Answer the phone, please, dear," Mrs. Carsen called.

Haley ran to the phone. Tori's mother appeared in the hallway. She seemed composed now. She smoothed her hair into place as she headed for the door. "I'll let Roger in," she told Haley.

Haley answered the phone. "Hello, Carsen residence."

"Hello," a woman replied. "This is Franny Wyatt calling from the Whitehall Hotel. I'd like to confirm arrangements for the Carsen-Arnold wedding reception. You're reserved for the twenty-third."

"Hang on," Haley said. "You'd better talk to Mrs. Carsen."

She put the phone down and stepped into the living room. Mrs. Carsen and Roger were sitting alone together on the couch, holding hands. Haley felt embarrassed, as if she were spying on them.

She cleared her throat. "Um, it's the Whitehall. They're calling to check your reservation."

Mrs. Carsen sighed tiredly. "I *can't* take one more

call today. Go ahead and confirm it, Haley. It's the twenty-third at five o'clock."

"Sure thing, Mrs. Carsen." Haley headed back to the phone. "Hello, Ms. Wyatt? The twenty-third is right."

"Good. Then I'll confirm your reservation for the twenty-third at six o'clock," Ms. Wyatt repeated.

"Right." Haley began to hang up. "No, wait!" she suddenly yelled. "It's not at six o'clock, it's at five o'clock!"

"Oh, I'm very sorry," Ms. Wyatt answered. "*Five* o'clock. It's a good thing you caught that." She chuckled.

"That's for sure!" Haley breathed a sigh of relief and hung up. Whew! That was a close call, she thought. If I made a mistake like that, the Carsens would never forgive me.

Because this is one wedding that has to be totally, absolutely perfect!

8. Jill

At a traditional wedding reception, the bride and groom lead the dancing. Many couples select a special song for this moment, for when the wedding is just a memory, music still has the ability to bring back powerful emotions.

—The Complete Wedding Book

" 'I can dream a thousand dreams, or make one of them come true,' " Jill sang out loud. " 'Yes, I can!' "

She stopped singing as she prepared for her next two jumps, a tuck axel and a triple toe loop. The lyrics of the song matched the spirit of the routine perfectly. Jill closed her eyes and imagined she was giving the performance of her life at Skate U.S.A. She soared into the air, completed the rotations, and landed both jumps effortlessly.

" 'I can fly to the top, I can reach for the stars, yes, I can!' " Singing again, she skimmed across the rink, preparing for the triple Lutz and triple salchow that came next.

She performed them gracefully, with energy to spare. She threw herself joyfully into a final sit spin and ended the routine with an extra flourish. " 'Yes, I can!' "

"Bravo!" Someone applauded loudly.

Jill spotted Ludmila standing at the boards. "You are really making progress," Ludmila called. "I'm not sure if the judges would add points for your singing performance. But your skating looks better than ever."

Jill felt her face flush. "I—I thought I was the only one in here."

"Which is why you were able to give such a flawless performance?" Ludmila raised an eyebrow. "Jill, if you can resist saving your best work for yourself, there will be quite a future for you. What I saw just now was impressive."

"Thank you." This time Jill flushed with pleasure.

"So." Ludmila's tone was businesslike again. "I have set the date of the test."

Jill felt her stomach jump nervously. She was more eager than ever to perform her routine at Skate U.S.A.

Ludmila reached into her warm-up jacket and removed a small datebook. "Eight o'clock on the twenty-fourth. You work well in the morning, Jill."

"Morning's great," Jill said. "Thank you, Ludmila." The twenty-fourth, she thought. Why does that sound so familiar? Then she remembered. Tori's mother's wedding was on the twenty-*third*. Oh, no! Jill thought.

"Um, Ludmila, that's *February* twenty-fourth, right?" she asked, just to be sure.

"Yes," Ludmila replied. "That leaves you about four weeks to prepare. That's not a problem, is it?"

"No, of course not," Jill told her. But now I can't *possibly* go to Tori's mother's wedding, she thought. She couldn't make it back to Colorado fresh for her test at eight o'clock the next morning. Tori would just have to understand.

Back in her dorm, Jill found a letter waiting for her on the hall table. She recognized Ryan's handwriting. Her heart leaped with happiness. She hadn't heard from him in two weeks. She raced upstairs to read the letter in the tub.

Ten minutes later Jill was stretched out in a tub full of cherry-scented bubble bath. Her long, straight black hair was tied up in a knot on top of her head. She unfolded Ryan's letter.

Dear Jill,

Hi. How are you? It snowed here yesterday. Too bad it was Saturday—we didn't get a day off from school! I guess you never get snow days, since you live at school. And they wouldn't let you have a day off from skating, anyway, right?

The bad part about the snow was that I had to shovel the whole driveway for my mom. It took about two hours. But afterward my friend Cynthia came over with this huge toboggan, and we went sledding over at Hunning's Hill.

Jill stopped reading. This was the second time in a row Ryan had written about Cynthia. Jill had never met her, but she knew Cynthia was in Ryan's class. She imagined Ryan and a beautiful high-school girl coasting down Hunning's Hill together on a sled. She felt sick.

Jill skimmed the rest of the letter, but there wasn't anything else about Cynthia. What should she do? She wanted to call Ryan right away, but she was afraid of what she might hear.

She stepped out of the tub and pulled on her terry-cloth robe. It's probably nothing, she told herself. Still, she suddenly wished she could go to Seneca Hills for the wedding. She needed to see Ryan again.

When Jill got back to her room, she found Bronya lying on her bed with her homework spread out in front of her. Playing on the tape deck was the music for Bronya's current routine—the theme from *Love Story*. The girls often took turns playing their skating music when they were in their room.

Bronya glanced up at her. "Jill, what's wrong?"

"I'm a little worried about something," Jill admitted.

Bronya sat up. "Is it Ludmila? She's still letting you take the senior levels, isn't she?"

Jill nodded. "Yes. Actually, I just saw her, and she told me she scheduled the test."

Bronya stared at her. "Then why do you look sad? Bad practice?"

Jill shook her head. "No. My skating's fine. It's the

rest of my life that's a mess." Jill sat down heavily on her bed. "Bronya, what would you think if your boyfriend started mentioning another girl?"

"Unless it was his sister, I would think it's time to give up on him," Bronya answered.

"Oh," Jill said. She paused. "Ryan mentioned this girl named Cynthia in his last two letters. They're probably just friends. But I can't help feeling jealous."

"Well, it's hard to stay boyfriend and girlfriend when you're thousands of miles apart," Bronya told her.

"It's not hard for *me*!" Jill protested. But even as she said it, she knew it wasn't true. It *was* hard. Still, she had stayed faithful to Ryan, and she expected the same from him.

There was a knock on the door. "Telephone, Jill!" called a voice.

"Maybe it's Ryan," she told Bronya. She hurried into the hall. "Hello?"

"Hi, Jill!"

"Tori!" Jill's heart sank.

"I'm calling to tell you how to take your measurements," Tori said. "Of course, the dresses would be a lot nicer without those stupid evening jackets Veronica talked my mother into. Oh, and speaking of jackets, did I tell you the latest thing Veronica did? You know my pink blazer? The really soft one with the gray trim?"

"I guess so," Jill said.

"I'm pretty sure Veronica borrowed it without asking me, and—"

"Tori, I have to ask you something," Jill interrupted. "It's about Ryan and his friend Cynthia."

"Oh, no! Don't say you want me to invite them. I can't ask everyone. But listen, Jill, I found the jacket hanging in a totally different spot in my closet. *Somebody* must have moved it, right? It had to have been Veronica," Tori concluded. "And now I'm missing my blue skirt! I bet she took that, too!"

Jill sighed. She'd been planning to ask Tori if she'd seen Ryan with Cynthia. But maybe it was better not to. Maybe she should write to Ryan about it first.

"And then today," Tori went on, "my mom and I were trying to pick out music for her first dance with Roger. Veronica kept butting in. She thinks she's a music expert. Anyway, we ended up picking this song called 'Our Love.' It's so pretty, I might use it for my next skating routine—"

"Speaking of skating," Jill interrupted, "I have to tell you something really important."

"What is it?" Tori asked.

Jill took a deep breath. "Ludmila thinks I'm ready to take the senior-level test," she blurted out.

Tori was silent a moment. "Oh," she said.

Jill could tell that Tori was jealous. "She scheduled me to take it on the morning of February twenty-fourth," Jill finished.

"But that's the morning after the wedding!" Tori exclaimed. "You'd never make it back in time for that!"

"I know," Jill admitted. She waited for Tori to start yelling. To her surprise, Tori's voice softened.

"Oh, Jill, you must feel so bad! You're going to have to miss it."

"I do feel bad, believe me. I know it's going to be a great wedding. I wish I could be there and see all of you—"

"What? Miss the wedding?" Tori sounded confused. "I thought you meant you'd miss the *test!*"

Jill's mouth dropped open in amazement. "Tori, we're talking about the senior-level test! This is *important.*"

"I know, but so is my mother's wedding. Isn't it?" Tori asked.

"Sure, but I can't pass up the test. I have to take it or I won't be able to compete in Skate U.S.A.," Jill argued.

"Jill, I'm counting on you," Tori said. "You have to be a bridesmaid. It will be terrible if it's just Haley and Veronica. Please, Jill! You said you'd do it!"

Jill tried to remember their last conversation. She knew she hadn't *refused* to be in the wedding, but she didn't think she had actually said she would do it, either. She hadn't even asked her parents about a plane ticket yet!

"Tell Ludmila you'll take the test some other time," Tori ordered. "There will be other competitions.

Come on, you and Haley are my best friends. You both have to be here for me!"

"But Tori—" Jill began.

"Anyway, I hope you can get a tape measure somewhere," Tori said, changing the subject.

Jill sighed. "I guess I can."

"Good," Tori said. "We need your waist, bust, hips, and height. I'll call you back for the measurements soon." She hung up.

Jill hung up and slumped down in the chair by the phone. She felt awful. The senior-level test was the most important thing in her skating life right now. But what about the rest of her life?

Tori *was* one of her best friends. And she was counting on Jill to be at the wedding. And then there was Ryan. What if he really was interested in Cynthia? If Jill went back for the wedding, she could find out for herself. What should she do?

Jill could hear music coming from her room. Bronya had switched the tape to Jill's music: "I can dream a thousand dreams, or make one of them come true!"

I *have* to make my dream come true, Jill told herself. But I can't give up everything else. Which do I choose? Skating . . . Ryan . . . or Tori's friendship?

9. Tori

The bride's chief helper is her maid of honor. To be chosen is truly a privilege and should be regarded as such. The maid of honor must strive to be companion and adviser, all at the same time! Above all, she should place the happiness of the bride and guests above her own.

—The Complete Wedding Book

"**I** felt that the seafood tarts were more elegant than the crab cakes, didn't you?" Mrs. Carsen steered the silver Jaguar down the winding driveway from the Circle Tower.

"Definitely," Tori agreed happily. She and her mother had just finished picking out the wedding menu. Tori was in a great mood. She had actually managed to help without Veronica butting in. It was the perfect time to ask a question that had been on her mind.

"Hey, Mom, how come Veronica doesn't have to go to school now?"

Mrs. Carsen cleared her throat. "She's on a break."

"We were just off for Christmas," Tori said. "What kind of school has another break in the middle of January?"

"I really don't know," Mrs. Carsen replied.

"It sounds kind of fishy," Tori insisted. "Veronica said all French schools have really long winter vacations."

"Well, then, there's your answer," her mother responded. "There's no need to go on discussing it." She pulled into a filling station. "We're low on gas."

Tori spotted a juice machine nearby. She felt in her pocket for some change. "I'm thirsty. I'll be back in a minute, Mom."

As Tori passed the self-serve island she spotted a guy bent over a car, pumping gas. His long brown hair seemed familiar. He turned, and she recognized Ryan McKensey, Jill's boyfriend.

"Hey, Ry—" Tori began. But she stopped herself when she spotted a girl with shoulder-length dark blond hair in the passenger seat of the car. As Tori watched, Ryan hurried back to the car. The girl smiled and leaned toward him. She placed a hand on his shoulder and whispered into his ear. Then she ruffled his hair. The car drove off.

Tori sucked in her breath. Was that Ryan's friend Cynthia? The one Jill had mentioned? Tori hoped not, because Cynthia sure had acted like more than a friend.

Tori opened her eyes long before her alarm sounded. Sometimes it was hard to get up so early in the morning! Tori groaned and forced herself to sit up. She hadn't slept well. She'd tossed and turned all night, thinking about the wedding . . . and about Ryan and Cynthia . . . and about her missing blue skirt.

The skirt was one of her favorites, and it had been gone for two days. The more Tori thought about it, the angrier she felt.

She jumped out of bed and threw on her robe. She really wanted to wear that skirt. So what if it was only four-thirty in the morning? If Veronica didn't want to be disturbed, she shouldn't go around taking people's clothes.

Tori marched into the hall. The house was silent. She pulled open the door to the guest room. Veronica was sound asleep, breathing noisily in the double bed. Tori switched on the light. To Tori's surprise, Veronica didn't budge. Her breathing remained loud and deep. Well, then, I'll just have to look for the skirt myself, Tori decided.

She yanked open the closet door and switched on the light. Veronica's clothes filled the space. There were shirts and pants and jackets and dresses in every color. Tori felt a pang of jealousy. Even her own closet wasn't this impressive. She searched quickly through the clothes. Her blue skirt was squashed into a corner. She snatched it up angrily.

Tori wondered what else Veronica might have borrowed without asking. She decided to check the bureau. There was just enough light spilling through the curtains from the streetlight outside to let her see.

The top drawer was filled with underwear, socks, and tights—none of them Tori's. She was about to close it when something caught her eye. A small red notebook was partly hidden under some clothes near the back. Tori glanced quickly at the bed to make sure Veronica was still sleeping. Then she slid out the notebook.

Tori opened the notebook, and a piece of yellow paper fell to the floor. She picked it up. It was a check, made out to the Académie Martine. It was signed *Adele Fouchard*. Tori shrugged and started to slip the check back in the notebook. As she did, one of the pages caught her eye. It was filled with signatures—Adele Fouchard's signatures. Some of them looked kind of funny. Tori studied the check and then the page again. With a start, she realized what she was looking at. Veronica had been trying to copy the signature. That was why she had practiced it over and over again.

Tori frowned. Veronica's last name was Fouchard. And her mother's name was Adele. Veronica was trying to copy her mother's signature! But what for?

There was a rustling sound coming from the bed. Tori quickly slipped the check back in the notebook and slid the book into the drawer. She had found her blue skirt. And something much better, too. The question was, how could she use it to get Veronica into really big trouble?

10. Jill

The perfect bridesmaid shows up on time and per-
forms her duties with good cheer. But most impor-
tant, she thinks of the wedding, and only the
wedding, until that most special day arrives.
                        —The Complete Wedding Book

I wonder what Cynthia looks like, Jill thought. She
pushed off with her left skate.

"Jill what are you doing?" Ludmila called. "I've
told you three times not to start with the left foot! Try
again. And this time, concentrate!"

"I'm sorry, Ludmila." Jill took her position again.
The afternoon practice was going terribly. Ludmila
was losing her patience, and Jill didn't blame her. Jill
knew she was making the same mistakes over and
over. But she couldn't help it. She just couldn't keep
her mind on skating.

Jill pushed forward with her right foot, preparing
for the triple toe loop.

Tori will be mad at me forever if I don't come to
the wedding, she thought. I bet even Mrs. Carsen will
be angry. I'll be letting everyone down.

Jill completed the triple toe loop and lifted into her next jump, a triple flip. She knew instantly that she didn't have the height she needed, but it was too late to stop. She tried rotating her shoulders extra hard. Instead of helping, though, the rotation threw her off balance. Jill crashed onto the ice with a thud. Tears of frustration and pain sprang to her eyes.

Ludmila stared at her with disapproval. "Tell me what you did wrong."

Jill stood up, brushed off her leggings, and forced her mind back to skating. "I stepped out before my weight was on the right foot. Then I tried to make up for it by rotating my shoulders too hard," she admitted.

"And you'll get a big bruise to remind you not to do it again," Ludmila finished. "You're making beginner's mistakes, Jill. I can't accept that. You must be ready for the test soon."

Jill stared at the ice. Ludmila would never understand what's bothering me, Jill realized. A serious skater puts skating first. Not boyfriends.

"We will have to end our session," Ludmila told her. "I must work with the other skaters. Work on your own now. I expect to see some improvement later today."

Jill nodded miserably. She tried the triple flip one more time. She didn't fall, but she didn't get very much height, either. She barely completed three rotations before landing.

"Hey, Jill!" someone called. Jill glanced up. Jesse Barrow stood at the boards. She skated over to him.

"Hey, Jill. How's it going?"

Jill forced a smile. "I'm not having a very good practice."

Jesse shrugged. "Maybe you're just a little worried about the senior levels."

That, and a few other things, Jill thought. She nodded. "I guess."

Jesse looked concerned. "Are you okay, Jill?"

Jill was tempted to tell Jesse everything—her worries about Tori and the wedding, even about Ryan and Cynthia. Would Jesse think she should stay and take the test or go back to Seneca Hills? But she stopped herself. After all, I barely know him, she reminded herself. "Yeah, I'm fine," she assured him.

"Jill!" Bronya hurried over to them. "I have messages for you. Tori called."

"She did?" Jill was filled with dread. Tori must want those measurements, she thought.

"And Ryan, too," Bronya went on.

"Ryan called?" Jill felt her stomach flip-flop. "Did he say what he was calling about?"

"No, but he said not to call back. He'll call you later," Bronya told her.

"I guess I'll be going," Jesse said quietly. "I have to get ready for a lesson."

Jill barely heard him. "Sure. Bye, Jesse." She turned to Bronya. "Are you sure he didn't want me to call back?"

Bronya shrugged. "That's what he said. But Tori definitely does want you to call her right away."

"Okay, sure." There was a phone near the locker room. Maybe, if she hurried, she could still catch Ryan. Her phone card was in her wallet in her locker.

Jill stepped off the ice and hurried to the locker room. Then she rushed to the phone to dial Ryan's number.

Ryan picked up right away. "Hello?"

Jill felt her throat tighten. "Hi," she said. "It's me."

"Jill?" Ryan sounded surprised to hear from her.

"Yeah. I got your message."

"But you weren't supposed to call back," Ryan said. "I mean, I'm about to go out. I can't really talk now."

"Oh." Jill felt a wave of disappointment.

"Hold on a minute, okay?" Jill heard muffled voices in the background. Ryan was talking to someone. Was that a girl's voice? Jill thought with a stab of panic. All of a sudden she wished she hadn't called Ryan at all.

Ryan returned to the phone. "Listen, I have to go right away. I'll call you back soon, okay?"

Jill swallowed. She felt sick. "Okay," she managed to answer. "Bye, Ryan."

Jill hung up the phone. What if Cynthia was the girl she'd heard talking at Ryan's house?

Slowly Jill made her way back to the rink. Jesse

was practicing with Matt Roe, one of the Academy coaches. Jill watched as Jesse performed a flawless double axel. Matt nodded approvingly. Jill wondered if Ludmila had noticed that she was gone. She slipped off her skate guards and stepped onto the ice again. But she couldn't stop thinking about the phone call. She felt anger welling up inside her.

Bronya slid to a stop in front of her, sending up a spray of ice. Her eyes were sparkling with excitement. "Jill, I have such good news," Bronya told her. "We're both preparing for the same thing!"

Jill was confused. "What?"

"The *test*," Bronya responded. "For the senior level. Ludmila said she wants me to take it as well." Bronya clutched Jill's arm. "We can go to Skate U.S.A. together!"

Jill forced a smile. "That's great, Bronya. I'm really happy for you." It was true. Jill *was* happy for her roommate. She knew how much skating at the senior level meant to Bronya.

But at the same time Jill felt added pressure. The skating world was competitive. If you didn't work to be the best, someone else would be ready to take your place. Jill didn't want Bronya to do better on the test than she did.

Too many things were going on at once, Jill thought. She wanted more than ever to go back to Seneca Hills now. She had to know if things were okay between her and Ryan. She had to know if she still had a boyfriend. But it was also important to stay in Denver and take the test. Wasn't it?

Jill pressed her hands against her head and moaned. Oh, if only I knew what to do!

11. Tori

The bride at a formal wedding usually carries a large bouquet, with smaller bouquets for the bridesmaids, and occasionally something special for the maid of honor. Although the bridesmaids' bouquets are small, they must still be special, for the bridesmaids must not in any way feel slighted by the larger role of the maid of honor.

—The Complete Wedding Book

Tori sat in the living room, leafing through *The Complete Wedding Book*. She hummed the tune to "Forever," the song from her skating routine. Her mother was due home soon. They were supposed to meet with the florist to discuss the wedding flowers.

There was a clattering on the stairs. Tori glanced up. Veronica was heading down to the living room. Tori ignored her, humming louder than ever. Veronica crossed the room and sat down at the piano. She began to play some scales.

"Do you mind?" Tori said in an irritated tone. "I'm trying to read." She went back to humming.

"Well, that's really too bad, because I have to practice now," Veronica responded. "Maybe you should go in your room if you want to read." She went back to her scales for a moment, then paused and switched to a song.

Tori realized that it was "Forever," the song she had been humming. But the way Veronica played it was especially annoying. She added lots of extra notes and fancy flourishes to the tune. Tori glared at Veronica, who was swaying back and forth to the music with her eyes closed. What a show-off, she thought.

Then Tori smiled to herself, remembering the little secret she had discovered the other day in Veronica's dresser drawer. Tori had been tempted many times since that morning to tell her mother about the notebook—and the forged signatures. Finally her mother would see that Veronica wasn't the angel she pretended to be. And then Veronica would be out of Tori's life forever!

But Tori knew it was best to find out *exactly* what Veronica was up to first.

The telephone rang, and Tori hurried to answer it. It was her mother. "Hi, Tori. Listen, I'm running late. Helene, the florist, is supposed to be there in a few minutes."

"Don't worry, Mom," Tori assured her. "I can take care of things."

"Is Veronica with you?" her mother asked.

"Yes," Tori said. "But what difference does that make?"

"You two make Helene comfortable," Mrs. Carsen replied. "I'll be there as soon as I can."

Tori frowned. "I can talk to the florist alone, Mom. Oh, listen, by the way, there's this bouquet I saw in the wedding book that would be *perfect* for the maid of honor, and—"

"Tori, not now," her mother cut her off. "I have to go. Later, okay? Bye."

Tori hung up the phone and turned back toward the living room. She wished Veronica would stop playing "Forever." It was driving her crazy. Did Veronica have to take *everything* that was Tori's?

The doorbell rang, and Tori hurried to the door. A man in a blue and red uniform waited on the other side of the peephole. "Who is it?" she asked.

"Express Delivery. I have a package here for Corinne Carsen and Roger Arnold."

It must be a wedding present, Tori realized with excitement. The first to arrive. She flung open the door. The man held a clipboard. A large package rested at his feet. "Are you Corinne Carsen?" he asked.

"Oh, no, but that's okay," Tori responded, reaching for the package. "You can just leave it with me."

The man shook his head. "Sorry, not unless Corinne Carsen or Roger Arnold signs for it."

"Okay, I can sign," a voice behind Tori said. Tori whipped around. Veronica had left the piano and was standing in the doorway to the living room.

"Corinne Carsen?" the man asked.

"That's right." Veronica stepped to the doorway. "Where do I sign?"

Tori gaped at her in amazement. "What are you doing?"

Veronica glared at her. "I'm *signing* for my *package*."

Tori watched in astonishment as Veronica scribbled Mrs. Carsen's name on the clipboard. "Okay," the man said, handing her the package. "Have a good evening."

When the man was gone, Veronica turned to Tori with a smile. "What do you think it is? Should we open it?"

"No, we should *not*," Tori responded. "And you shouldn't have signed for it, either, Veronica."

"Oh, come on, Tori," Veronica said. "People do that all the time."

"You mean *you* do it all the time," Tori shot back.

Veronica's face paled. "What are you talking about?"

Tori hesitated. The doorbell rang again. *"I'll* get it," Tori announced. She opened the door to a small woman with short brown hair. She wore round glasses and carried a green canvas bag. "Hello. I'm Helene Murray, the florist," she introduced herself.

"Hi, come on in," Tori said. "My mom's going to be a little late."

Veronica glided forward. "Yes, please come in. May I take your coat?"

"Why, yes, thank you." Helene slipped off her gray raincoat and handed it to Veronica.

Veronica shoved the coat at Tori and sailed toward

the living room. "Please make yourself at home. I'm sure Corinne will be here as soon as she can."

"Hey!" Tori threw the coat onto the hall table and hurried into the living room.

Helene was perched on the white couch. Veronica leaned over her. "May I get you something to drink?"

Tori marched over to them. "*I'll* get you something. We have iced tea, ginger ale—"

"Iced tea would be fine," Helene answered. "Thank you."

"Yes, thank you, Tori," Veronica echoed. "You can bring me one, too, please." She sat down beside Helene on the couch. Tori gaped at her. "Tori," Veronica scolded, "don't just stand there. Our guest is thirsty."

Tori stormed into the kitchen. She yanked open the refrigerator door and grabbed the pitcher of iced tea. There's no way I'm getting *anything* for Veronica, Tori told herself. She hastily poured some tea into a crystal glass, spilling some on the counter.

When she hurried back to the living room, she was surprised to find her mother there, shaking off her cashmere coat. "I hope you haven't waited too long, Helene," Mrs. Carsen said. "I got tied up. Have the girls been keeping you company?"

"Oh, yes, thank you," Helene responded.

Tori handed Helene her drink. "Here you go."

"Hi, sweetheart." Mrs. Carsen planted a kiss on Tori's cheek. "Oh, that tea looks wonderful. Would you get me a glass, please?" She sank onto the couch next to Helene. Tori headed wordlessly back toward the kitchen.

"Don't forget mine, okay, Tori?" Veronica called after her.

Tori slammed two glasses down on the counter. She filled one glass and began to pour the second. The tea ran out when the glass was less than half full. Well, that's all Veronica's getting, Tori thought. She carried the glasses back to the living room and set them down on the coffee table.

Mrs. Carsen and Veronica were sitting on either side of Helene. Tori stood in front of Veronica, waiting for her to give up her seat. Helene opened a brochure. "I thought we'd choose the bouquets first," she announced.

Tori cleared her throat. Veronica glanced up at her. "Oh, thanks," Veronica said, reaching for her tea.

"Where am *I* supposed to sit?" Tori asked.

Mrs. Carsen raised her eyes from the brochure for a moment. "Tori, just sit anywhere," she said impatiently. "There are plenty of seats in this room."

Tori threw herself down in a white armchair. She glared at Veronica, but Veronica was busy studying the brochure and didn't notice.

"Will the attendants carry bouquets?" Helene asked.

"Yes," Tori answered. "And shouldn't mine be different from the others, since I'm the maid of honor? I like this." She reached for *The Complete Wedding*

Book and showed her mother and Helene a photo of a pink, purple, and white arrangement.

"Oh, that won't work at all," Veronica said, peering at the picture.

"Nobody asked *you*," Tori replied.

"Tori," her mother reprimanded. "Don't be rude."

Veronica examined the photo closely. "Isn't that a *bride's* bouquet?"

"So?" Tori asked. "I'm the maid of honor. That's almost as important as the bride."

Helene frowned. "Well, I suppose we *could* highlight the maid of honor's bouquet with a few of the same flowers I'm using in the bridal bouquet."

"That sounds lovely," Mrs. Carsen declared. She smiled at Tori. Tori forced herself to smile back.

Helene told Mrs. Carsen her ideas for the rest of the wedding flowers. Tori sat in silence. Why should I say anything when no one's going to listen to me anyway? Tori reasoned. Finally Helene stood up to leave. Mrs. Carsen saw her to the door, and Veronica and Tori trailed behind.

"Good-bye, Helene, and thank you," Mrs. Carsen called. Then she turned and spotted the package resting by the door. "Oh, what's this?"

"It came a little while ago," Veronica volunteered. "I thought it might be a wedding present, since it's addressed to you and Roger."

This was Tori's chance. "That's right," she put in. "It *is* addressed to you and Roger, Mom. But *Veronica* signed for it."

Mrs. Carsen turned to Veronica. "Oh, thank you, Veronica." She picked up the package. "Our first gift. I wonder what it is. I suppose I should wait for Roger."

Tori stared at her mother in astonishment. "Mom, didn't you hear what I said? The delivery man said you or Roger had to sign. Veronica forged your name!"

"Oh, Tori, please." Mrs. Carsen's tone was exasperated. "There's nothing wrong with having someone else sign for a package if I'm not around."

Tori had planned on telling her mother about Veronica's notebook, but now she wasn't so sure she should. Mrs. Carsen seemed ready to let Veronica get away with anything—even faking other people's signatures. With Tori's luck, *she'd* probably be the one who got in trouble, for snooping through Veronica's stuff!

"I'm going up to my room," Tori announced. "I have homework." As she bounded up the stairs she heard Veronica speaking to her mother in that fake sweet voice. Tori paused to listen.

"Corinne, thank you for letting me be part of all this," Veronica said. "You know, my mother and I have never really been close. In some ways I'm starting to feel like you're the mom I never had. I'm honored that you made me a bridesmaid."

"I want you to feel like a member of the family while you're here, Veronica," her mother responded.

A member of the family! Veronica has *taken over* the family, Tori thought.

"Well, I know Tori is proud to be your maid of honor," Veronica went on. "I just wish there was some special place for me. A way I could show everyone at the wedding how you've taken me in. I'm practically your *other* daughter."

What is she talking about? Tori wondered with alarm. Veronica doesn't expect my mom to let *her* be a maid of honor, too, does she? Tori started back down the stairs. Mom can't let her do that! she thought. I'll quit the wedding if she does!

After two furious steps Tori paused. That's probably just what Veronica wants! Tori realized. She wants me to quit and let her be the only maid of honor. Well, I'm not going to let *that* happen! Tori declared to herself.

She turned and raced upstairs. She grabbed the telephone in her mother's room and began to dial Haley's number. She stopped suddenly and hung up. Haley was Tori's friend, but she always seemed to take Veronica's side. Besides, Haley didn't understand how important the wedding was to Tori. She would probably think it was fine for Veronica to be a maid of honor.

Tori decided to call Jill. Jill hadn't called back with her measurements yet, anyway. But Jill sounded disappointed when she answered the phone.

"Oh, hi, Tori, it's you," Jill said. "I was hoping it might be Ryan. He's supposed to call me back."

With a pang, Tori remembered spotting Ryan with that other girl. Tori had told Haley and Nikki about it at practice, and together they had decided not to tell Jill.

Still, Tori felt bad about keeping the secret. She quickly changed the subject. "Jill, do you have your measurements? My mom's seamstress really needs them to start on your dress."

Jill sighed. "Sorry, I completely forgot about them."

"What are you talking about?" Tori asked. "Doesn't anyone take me seriously anymore?"

"Sorry. I've just been so worried about the senior levels," Jill explained. "Ludmila is putting tons of pressure on me, and—"

"Oh, so Ludmila means more to you than I do," Tori said in a hurt voice.

"No! It's not like that," Jill tried to explain. "You understand how she is, Tori."

"I understand that you don't care about what's important to me," Tori replied.

"That's not true. But you know how important this test is to *me*," Jill tried again.

"Of *course* I know. Or did you forget that you're not the only serious skater from Seneca Hills?" Tori's voice rose.

"I didn't mean it that way," Jill protested.

"Well, you'd better get those measurements," Tori warned her. "Or else your friends here are going to think that you deserted them. And I'm not just talking about your *girl*friends," she added.

"What do you mean? What are you talking about?" Jill's voice trembled.

Tori knew she had said too much. But she couldn't help herself. Her feelings were hurt. "I mean it might be a good idea for you to check up on your boyfriend."

"Do you know something about Ryan that I don't?" Jill asked in a panic. "Tell me, Tori."

"Why don't you just come back and see for yourself? *If* you can take time away from your skating," Tori added. She slammed down the phone.

Immediately Tori felt terrible. She knew Jill was really upset. She shouldn't have said anything to Jill about Ryan. Tori suddenly wished Jill *wouldn't* listen seriously to what she'd said!

12. Haley

A formal wedding calls for formal, engraved invitations that include the date, time, and location of the big event. But they also serve as cherished mementos after the wedding. Some family and guests will request extra invitations to keep long after the wedding has passed.

—The Complete Wedding Book

Haley adjusted the angle of the sit-up board. She locked her ankles into place and lay flat, with her head close to the ground. "Okay, here goes. Thirty-five sit-ups," she promised herself.

Haley and the other members of Silver Blades were required to work out in the weight room at the rink. It was important to strengthen their muscles for skating. Haley had arrived early and had the weight room to herself. "One, two, three . . . ," she began counting.

As she reached twenty-seven a familiar-looking pair of legs in an electric blue unitard stopped in front of her. "Hey, Haley," Tori's voice called from above.

"Twenty-eight, twenty-nine. Hi, Tori," Haley responded. "How's everything?"

"Terrible," Tori complained.

"Let me guess," Haley said. "Thirty-two, thirty-three, thirty-four. Veronica again, right?"

"And Jill, too," Tori added.

Haley paused. "Jill!" she exclaimed in surprise. "What did *she* do?"

"She's trying to get out of being a bridesmaid," Tori reported.

"That doesn't sound like Jill." Haley frowned. "Thirty-five," she said, finishing her last sit-up. "Why?"

"It doesn't matter why," Tori answered. "What matters is that I need her here. I need *all* my friends with me. Especially now that Veronica's trying to take my place."

"Tori, what are you talking about?" Haley asked.

"I heard her talking to my mother all about it last night," Tori reported. Her voice was shaking. "Veronica was going on and on about how she's my mom's *other* daughter now. She wants to be a maid of honor in the wedding, too." Tori looked as if she was about to cry.

"Oh, wow. Are you sure?" Haley asked. She knew how much being maid of honor meant to Tori. "I mean, you and your mom are so close. Your mom would never agree to something like that. Would she?"

"You tell me," Tori said. "This morning, in the car, my mom said she's taking Veronica for an extra fitting this afternoon. I bet she's going to tell Zophia to make Veronica a dress like mine. What else could it be?"

"Well, it wouldn't be the end of the world. Anyway, maybe Zophia just needs to check Veronica's measurements," Haley suggested.

"You always take Veronica's side!" Tori burst out.

"Tori, that's not true," Haley objected. "I know you don't like Veronica, but sometimes you get a little carried away about her."

"Oh, yeah? Then wait until I tell you about the notebook," Tori said.

"What notebook?" Haley asked.

"I found it in her room," Tori explained. "There was a check in it, signed by her mother. And a whole page where Veronica was practicing her mother's signature."

Haley was astonished. "Really?"

Tori nodded. "I don't know what she's up to, but that's *forgery*," she said. "And I bet there's other stuff in that notebook that I should know about. Which is why I need your help."

"Me?" Haley blinked. "What do you want *me* to do?"

"My mom wants me to stop by the printer's today to check on the wedding invitations," Tori explained. "But that's when she and Veronica will be at Zophia's. It's the perfect time for me to sneak back into the guest room and go through the notebook. So I need *you* to go to the printer's for me."

"I don't know, Tori." Haley was doubtful. "Maybe you should just tell your mom about all of this."

"I can't," Tori told her. "My mom thinks Veronica can do no wrong. Don't you see? I have to find more proof that Veronica's up to something bad."

"Oh, all right," Haley agreed. "This does seem important. I'll go to the printer's."

"Great. Just make sure the invitation says the right things," Tori explained. "My mom wrote it all down for me. I'll give it to you. If the invitations are all right, just tell the printer to go ahead. But get him to give you one invitation right away. I want to send it to Jill."

"Jill? I thought you just said she didn't want to come," Haley said.

"That's *exactly* why I need to send an invitation right away," Tori said. "Don't you see? Once Jill gets that invitation in the mail, it will be harder for her to say no."

Later that day Haley stood at the counter in the printing shop, examining an invitation. It was pink with a maroon border. Haley compared the information on the invitation to the information on the slip of paper Tori had given her.

I wish Tori hadn't asked me to do this, Haley thought. What if I mess it up? Mrs. Carsen will be furious.

Corinne Francine Carlyle Carsen

and Roger Matthew Arnold

request the honor of your presence

on the occasion of their marriage

at four o'clock on the afternoon of

February twenty-seventh

at the Chapel by the Lake, Seneca Hills

Reception to follow at the Whitehall Hotel

"You can take this invitation to Mrs. Carsen," the printer told her. "I'll print up two hundred and fifty copies. Tell her they'll be ready tomorrow."

"Wait a minute! This is supposed to say February twenty-*third*," Haley told him. "It says February twenty-*seventh*. That's a huge mistake!"

"Oh, look at that." The printer peered at the card. "You see, that's why we have folks come in and check these things before we print up the final copies. I'll make up a new one right now." He left Haley with the old invitation and hurried to the back of his shop.

A few minutes later he reappeared with another pink and maroon card. The date on this one had been changed to February twenty-third.

"That's better," Haley said with relief. "It's a good

thing that I spotted that mistake. Mrs. Carsen would have a fit if the date was wrong."

"I wouldn't blame her," the printer agreed.

"Oh, and one more thing," Haley said. "Can you print up an extra one of these for me right now?"

"Sure. Another minute," the printer told her. While Haley waited, she pulled out the envelope Tori had given her. It already had a stamp attached and Jill's address written across it. All Haley had to do now was drop the invitation in the mail, so that Jill would receive it right away.

A few minutes later the man returned with the new invitation. Haley grabbed all three copies and headed for the mailbox outside the print shop. As she walked she slid the invitation into the envelope and sealed the flap.

That's over and done with, she said to herself as the envelope disappeared into the mail slot. I'll tell Tori everything went great. Though I don't see how mailing Jill an invitation is going to change her mind about coming to the wedding. I know Jill. Once she makes up her mind, nothing can change it!

13. Jill

A wedding should be a time of joy, not worry. Which is why, whenever possible, expenses for the wedding party should be the responsibility of the bride's family.

—The Complete Wedding Book

"Come on, Jill. You can't sit here all evening," Bronya declared. "Let's go to the party at Glacier House."

"I'm not in the mood for a party," Jill said, her nose in her math book. "But thanks anyway."

"You will be once you get there," Bronya insisted. "Even my coach back in Romania said it's not good to work all the time. You need some play now and then."

Jill closed her math book and sat up on her bed. "Well, I'm not really working much," she admitted.

"Still worried about Ryan?" Bronya asked with concern.

Jill nodded. "Bronya, it's been a week and he still hasn't called back. Do you think it's because he's with Cynthia?"

Bronya folded her arms across her chest. "If he is, then he doesn't deserve to have you worrying about him. That's all the more reason for you to go out." She smiled. "I bet Jesse will be at Glacier House."

"Jesse's just a friend," Jill told her.

"Because that's all you *let* him be," Bronya pointed out. "Jill, open your eyes! There are great boys right here."

"But what if Ryan's still my boyfriend?" Jill asked.

Bronya shrugged. "Does having a boyfriend mean that you can't go to a party here at school?"

"No, I guess not," Jill admitted.

"So then come on," Bronya urged. "We'll go together." She pulled Jill up from the bed.

"Okay, okay," Jill said, managing a little laugh.

She and Bronya made their way downstairs and headed toward the door. Lisa Welch, the dorm parent at Aspen House, called out to them. "Jill, hold on."

"Hi, Lisa," Jill greeted her. "Bronya and I are going to the party at Glacier House, okay?"

"That's fine." Lisa hurried toward them. "I just wanted to give you some mail. It came this afternoon." She handed Jill a fancy square envelope.

There was no return address, but the postmark was from Seneca Hills. Jill felt her heart give a little leap. Maybe it was from Ryan! She tore open the envelope. But all that was inside was an invitation to Mrs. Carsen's wedding.

"It's beautiful," Bronya commented, leaning over to peer at the pink and maroon card. "What is it?"

"The invitation to Tori's mother's wedding," Jill told her. "Too bad I can't go." She read through the invitation. "Wait a minute!" She examined the card again. "This says the wedding's on the twenty-*seventh*, not the twenty-third. That's three days *after* the senior-level test!" Jill let out a cry of joy. "I must have gotten the date wrong when Tori told me."

Jill's mind was racing. Now she *could* go back to Seneca Hills—even if it meant paying her parents back for the plane ticket herself, a little at a time.

"Bronya," she said, "I'm sorry, but I can't go to that party with you. I have to find Ludmila right away." A big smile spread across her face. "I *can* go to the wedding after all!"

A little while later Jill paused outside the door to Ludmila's cottage. Jill knew Ludmila didn't like to be disturbed during her time off. But this was important. Jill needed to clear her visit home right away. Jill took a deep breath and knocked on the door.

Ludmila answered the door wearing glasses. Jill had never seen her coach wearing them before.

"Jill, is everything all right?" Ludmila asked.

"Yes," Jill assured her, "everything's fine. I'm sorry to disturb you, but I need to talk to you about something."

"Well, then, come in." Ludmila stepped back, and Jill followed her inside. Jill had never seen the inside of Ludmila's cottage before. It was cozily furnished, with a large blue plaid couch and a thick blue rug. Framed photographs of Ludmila and other skaters in action hung from the wood-paneled walls. In the corner stood a huge oak desk, covered with papers. The desk light was on, and a gigantic black cat crouched on top of the papers.

"Vanya, get down!" Ludmila commanded, waving at the cat. The cat started to lick its paw. Ludmila shook her head. "You see, he does what he likes. So, Jill, what is it you wish to see me about?"

Jill cleared her throat. "I was wondering if I could go back to Seneca Hills after the senior-level test," she began. "Just for a few days."

"Is everything all right with your family?" Ludmila asked.

"Yes," Jill assured her. "It's just that there's a wedding on the twenty-seventh. I'm supposed to be a bridesmaid. And I could probably get in some practice time at my old rink with Silver Blades." Jill waited hopefully.

Ludmila tilted her head, thinking. "Perhaps a change of scenery would be good for you. It might even help you feel refreshed for Skate U.S.A. All right, Jill, you may go. But only for a few days. And you must skate while you are there."

"Thanks, Ludmila." Jill was so grateful. She was going back to Seneca Hills! She couldn't wait to call Tori!

She raced back to Aspen House and dialed Tori's number. An unfamiliar person answered the phone. "Hello?"

"Hello, may I please speak to Tori?" Jill asked.

"Just a minute." A moment later Tori came on.

"Hi, Tori, it's me," Jill said. "Guess what? I'm coming!"

"To the wedding?" Tori's voice was full of excitement. "Do you have your measurements?"

Jill laughed. "No, I forgot. But I'll get them soon."

"This is great!" Tori paused. "But what about the test?"

"You won't believe this, but I had the date wrong the whole time," Jill told her. "I guess I wasn't paying attention. The wedding is three days *after* my test!"

"That's fantastic," Tori said. "I really need you here, Jill." She lowered her voice. "I can't talk much now, because Veronica's in the next room."

"Did you find your skirt, or whatever it was you thought she took?" Jill asked.

"Yes," Tori whispered. "And I found something else—a notebook with forged signatures. It's a long story. But I know she's up to something. I sneaked back into her room the other day to try to find the notebook again, but she must have hidden it somewhere else. Oops, here she comes." Tori's voice grew much louder. "So, *Jill*, I can't *wait* to see you. We're going to have *so* much *fun* when you get here."

Jill laughed into the phone. "Tori, you are a terrible actress."

Tori returned to her normal tone. "Seriously,

though, Jill, I'm really glad you're coming.'' She hesitated. "And I'm sorry I blew up on Monday. I shouldn't have hung up on you.''

"That's okay, Tori," Jill assured her. "You were upset. We both were." Jill paused. "But I have to ask you what you meant about Ryan.''

"Oh, that. It was nothing, Jill, really. I shouldn't have said anything.''

"Tori, come on," Jill said. "I know that's not true. Tell me.''

Tori was silent for a moment. "Okay. But it wasn't a big deal. I just saw Ryan driving around with some girl. It was probably nothing. They're probably just friends.''

Jill felt as if someone had punched her in the stomach. "No, Tori, I don't think so." She swallowed hard. "Ryan's been talking about this girl named Cynthia in his letters. And when he called here the other day, I wasn't around, and he left a message saying not to call him back. I did anyway, and I heard a girl talking in the background. I bet it was Cynthia! I bet that's who you saw him with!''

"Oh, wow. Listen, Jill," Tori began. "The best thing is to just come back here. Then you can see for yourself if anything's going on. Don't even tell Ryan you're coming. You can surprise him and find out for sure.''

"Yeah," Jill agreed. "That makes sense. I'd better get off the phone, though. I need to call my parents and tell them I'm coming home.'' Jill wasn't looking forward to the call. She really felt bad about asking her parents for the ticket.

"Well, okay. I'll tell my mom to call her travel agent," Tori added.

"Tori, my mom works in a travel agency," Jill reminded her. "She can reserve a plane ticket for me."

"Why would she do that?" Tori asked. "My mom's travel agent has to bill it to her account."

"What?" Jill could hardly believe her ears. "Your *mother* is paying for my ticket?"

"Of course," Tori responded. "The bride pays for the bridesmaids to get to the wedding. And for their dresses, too. Everyone knows that."

"I didn't! Are you sure it's okay?" Jill was doubtful. "It's pretty expensive."

"It's nothing compared to how much some stuff for the wedding costs," Tori assured her. "The wedding cake probably costs more than your ticket and the dress put together."

"Oh, Tori, this is great!" Jill felt excited and nervous all at once. I'm going home for the wedding! she thought. And Ryan is going to get the surprise of his life.

14. Tori

Choosing a gift for a bride and groom who have both been married before can be a challenge, especially if each already has a well-stocked household. Traditional gifts such as china and table linens are probably not appropriate. A second-time bride and groom will appreciate the extra effort that goes into finding a truly unusual gift.

— The Complete Wedding Book

A loud beep sounded in Tori's ears. Her alarm clock! She rolled over and pulled her pillow over her head. Her room was completely dark. She wished she could sleep for just a few more minutes before she had to get up for practice.

Then she remembered—she had set her alarm extra early that morning. She was going to sneak into the guest room again to look for Veronica's notebook. Tori had searched for the notebook every chance she got, but with no luck. Veronica must be taking it with her wherever she went.

Tori knew she'd have to try snooping while Veronica was home. Which meant sneaking in there while Veronica was still asleep. But Veronica was a pretty heavy sleeper. Tori had learned that when she sneaked into the guest room to get her blue skirt. And Veronica was never up this early.

Tori reached for the flashlight she had slipped under her bed the night before. She pulled on her light blue robe and stepped quietly into the hall. Veronica might be a heavy sleeper, but Mrs. Carsen wasn't. Tori didn't want to explain what she was doing up before dawn with a flashlight in her hand, headed for the guest room.

Tori crept across the hall and silently pushed open Veronica's door. Her heart was pounding as she aimed the beam of the flashlight around the room. Where would Veronica have hidden that notebook? Tori tiptoed across the room—and realized that she didn't hear Veronica's heavy breathing. She froze. What if Veronica was lying awake, watching her?

Tori swung the flashlight toward the bed. It was empty!

Tori stared at the bed in shock. It was practically the middle of the night. Where was Veronica?

Tori suddenly realized that this was her big chance. She could really get Veronica in trouble now. Mrs. Carsen had strict curfews for Tori and Veronica. She'd be furious that Veronica had sneaked out in the middle of the night. Finally she'd see Veronica for what she really was! She might even send her back to France that very day!

Tori rushed down the hall to her mother's room. "Mom! Mom!" she cried. "Wake up, quick!"

Tori's mother sat up and yawned. "What is it?" she asked.

"Veronica," Tori nearly shouted. "She's gone. She's not in her bed."

"*What?*" Tori's mother flung off her covers. "Are you sure?"

"Go see for yourself," Tori answered. "She must have sneaked out in the middle of the night."

Mrs. Carsen threw on her white silk robe and walked quickly down the hall. Tori followed closely behind. She could barely keep a smile off her face. They arrived at the guest room, and Mrs. Carsen switched on the overhead light. "Oh, my goodness," she cried.

"I guess she's in pretty big trouble, huh?" Tori asked.

"Oh, I hope not," Mrs. Carsen turned to Tori. "Have you checked downstairs?"

"No." Tori was disappointed. She expected her mother to be angry. Instead, her mom actually seemed worried.

Mrs. Carsen flew downstairs with Tori at her heels. The living room and kitchen were dark and empty. She switched on the kitchen light. "We'd better call Roger."

Now we're getting somewhere, Tori thought with satisfaction. Mrs. Carsen picked up the kitchen phone. As she put the receiver to her ear, her expression changed. "Hello?" She paused. "*Veronica? Is that you?*"

Tori stared at her mother, confused. "Veronica's on the *phone*?"

A moment later Veronica waltzed into the kitchen, heading out of the room Mrs. Carsen used as a study. Tori gaped at her. "What are you doing down here?"

Tori's mother hung up the phone. "Veronica," she sighed. "You had us so worried!"

"I'm sorry, Corinne," Veronica said in her fake sweet voice. "I just came down here to make a phone call."

"Yes, well, I recognized your voice when I picked up the extension," Mrs. Carsen said. "But who were you calling at this hour?"

Veronica glanced at them both, then licked her lips. "Well, actually, I—I—" she stammered.

"This had better be good," Tori muttered under her breath.

Veronica glanced down at the floor. "Well, the thing is, I can't really tell you."

Tori grinned. This was it! This was the moment she'd been waiting for! "You'd *better* tell us," she ordered.

"Tori," Mrs. Carsen said sharply, "I'll handle this." She turned to Veronica. "Well?" she asked.

"But . . . but it was about your *present*," Veronica said. "It's something special that I wanted to order for you and Roger. That's why I didn't want you to know about the call."

Tori's mother's face softened. "Oh, Veronica! You

don't need to get us a wedding gift. Especially one that you have to go to so much trouble for."

"But I really want you and Roger to know how much I appreciate everything you've done for me," Veronica told her.

"Oh, come *on*," Tori scoffed. "You're not going to fall for that, are you, Mom?"

"Tori, really," Mrs. Carsen scolded. "Veronica is our guest. It's time you started being a little more civil to her."

"Me?" Tori cried in disbelief. "She's the one who sneaked out of bed in the middle of the night. I can't believe *I'm* the one who's getting in trouble!"

"Tori, that's enough," Mrs. Carsen said. She glanced at the kitchen clock. "You'd better get ready for practice now. Veronica, you should go back to bed. And forget all about this present idea."

Veronica left the kitchen without a word.

"Wow," Danielle commented. "Veronica sounds amazing."

Tori nodded. She and her friends hurried through the crowd of Saturday shoppers at the mall. They were searching for a special wedding gift for Roger and Mrs. Carsen. Tori had just finished telling them about Veronica's secret phone call.

"I think she's mean," Nikki said. "Of course, I met her only once, at the rink."

"Do you think she could be telling the truth about the present?" Martina asked.

"I don't know," Tori admitted. "But I'm not taking any chances. If Veronica *does* get my mom and Roger a present, I know it'll be something incredible."

"How come?" Danielle asked.

Martina rolled her eyes. "You should see her clothes. She's like something out of a magazine."

"She does have great taste," Haley agreed. "Tori even said so."

Tori sighed. "Yeah. I bet she'll think of the perfect gift for Mom and Roger. And that's why I have to get them something even better."

"Better than perfect?" Haley shook her head. "That sounds pretty tough."

"That's why you're all here," Tori said. "I told you, I need all five of us to search the mall together. We're bound to come up with something terrific, right?"

But two hours later they hadn't come up with a thing. Tori threw herself down on a bench outside Sports Sensations.

"I can't believe it," she said. "We've been to practically every store in the mall. And there was nothing special enough to buy."

"Well, I liked that vase at Roselle's," Danielle said. "But I guess it wasn't very special."

"And I loved those matching robes from La Chic Boutique. But I guess that would be an ordinary present, too," Nikki said.

Everyone agreed. Nothing had seemed good enough. "What will I do?" Tori frowned.

"I guess you'll have to go shopping again," Haley told her.

"I guess." Tori's shoulders sagged. "But whatever I get, I just know Veronica will find something even better."

15. Jill

~~~~~~~~~~

It is considered appropriate for the bride's family to treat the bride's attendants as if they were also members of the family—at least while preparations are being made, and up to the time of the wedding itself.
—The Complete Wedding Book

Jill ripped open the thick envelope. "It's here! My plane ticket for the wedding!" She felt like kissing the envelope.

Jill had been much more cheerful for the past week—ever since she learned that she could go back to Seneca Hills. Her family was thrilled that she was coming home for another visit. And Jill couldn't wait to see them, either. If only she had heard from Ryan, everything would be perfect.

Jill scanned the ticket: *Air America, flight 32, depart Denver, Colorado, 3:15 P.M., February 19. Return from Seneca Hills 7:30 P.M., February 24.*

"What?" Jill studied the ticket again. "February nineteenth to February twenty-fourth? There must be some mistake!"

"What is it? What's wrong?" Bronya glanced up from her desk.

"The wedding is on the twenty-*seventh*," Jill told her. "This ticket doesn't make any sense."

Jill rushed to her desk. A feeling of dread was growing in her stomach. Jill searched frantically through her papers. "I *know* I put it in here." She dug out the wedding invitation. Sure enough, it said February twenty-seventh.

"Something's wrong. I hope it's the ticket," Jill said. The ticket showed that Jill would return to Colorado on the night of the twenty-fourth. But Ludmila had scheduled Jill's test for the *morning* of the twenty-fourth.

"I've got to call Tori." Jill raced into the hall, grabbed the phone, and dialed Tori's number. "Hello," Jill said quickly. "Is Tori there?"

"No, she isn't," a girl's voice answered. "Do you want to leave a message?"

"Is this Veronica?" Jill asked.

"Yes," the girl said. "Who's this?"

"My name's Jill Wong," Jill explained. "I'm one of Tori's friends, but I go to school in Colorado now."

"Yes?" Veronica said, a trace of impatience in her voice.

"Anyway, I'm supposed to be in the wedding," Jill went on hurriedly. "You know, when Mrs. Carsen marries Mr. Arnold?"

"Oh, right. You're the one who couldn't come for any fittings," Veronica said.

"Yeah, I guess," Jill said. "Anyway, I'm just wondering, could you tell me when it is? The wedding, I mean?"

Veronica burst out laughing. "You must be kidding! You're supposed to be a bridesmaid and you don't even know when it is?"

"Well, see, I have this invitation," Jill told her, "but it says February twenty-seventh."

"The twenty-seventh? That's not right," Veronica said. "Corinne and Roger are getting married on the twenty-third."

"Oh." Jill felt sick. "Are you sure?"

"Of course I'm sure," Veronica snapped. "I'm in the wedding, too, you know. I don't know where you got that invitation, but it's wrong, Julie."

"*Jill*," Jill corrected her.

"Whatever," Veronica said. "Anyway, the wedding's on the twenty-third. Is there anything else you wanted to know?" .

Jill swallowed. "No, I guess not." She hung up the phone with her heart sinking. This was awful. Jill couldn't possibly tell Tori that she couldn't come for the wedding. Not now. She'd promised Tori she'd be there for sure.

Besides, her ticket was already bought. And from what Veronica said, it sounded as if Jill's dress was already being made. And what about my family? Jill thought. They're counting on seeing me! And Ryan—this might be my only chance to find out what's going on with him.

Jill squared her shoulders. She had to talk to Ludmila. Jill was terrified of telling her coach about the mixup. But what else could she do?

16. Tori

Four or five days before the wedding, things are generally well in hand. The refreshments and flowers have been ordered. The band has been hired. And, most important, the bridal gown and attendants' dresses are safely on hand while all wait for the special day to arrive.

—The Complete Wedding Book

"There she is. There's Jill!" Tori waved wildly. She and Haley hurried across the airport waiting area. Jill rushed up to them, and the three girls hugged.

"Jill, you look great," Tori said. "I knew you'd come!"

"How was the trip?" Haley asked.

"Great," Jill said. "Tori, did you know that ticket was first class?"

Tori shrugged. "My mom always flies first class. I guess the travel agent just figured she should make the usual arrangements."

"First class sounds cool," Haley said. "What was it like?"

"Fantastic," Jill told her. "They served shrimp cocktail and a fabulous dessert. Plus they gave me some really nice slippers that I got to keep. But the best thing is that Ludmila let me come."

Haley nodded. "I'm so glad she arranged for you to take the senior test here, with Kathy."

"Me too," Tori agreed. "I can't believe Haley sent you the wrong invitation!"

"Hey!" Haley punched Tori in the arm. "I can't believe *you* didn't tell me that Jill was going to take the senior-level test!"

Tori couldn't help feeling jealous that Jill was taking the test at Tori's own rink. She and Haley had talked about it the previous night. Tori had decided that she would work really hard on her skating *after* the wedding. That way she could take the test and catch up to Jill really quickly.

"The important thing is that you're here," Tori told Jill.

A man in a dark jacket stepped up to Tori. "Do you have any bags to pick up?" he asked.

"My mom hired a car for us," Tori explained to Jill. "This is the driver."

Jill shook her head. She held up her duffel bag. "This is all I brought." She and the others followed the driver out to the car. They settled into the wide backseat, and the car took off toward Seneca Hills.

"It's great to be home," Jill said. "Though I am a little worried about seeing Ryan."

"You didn't tell him you were coming, did you?" Tori asked.

"No." Jill shook her head.

"Good. Let's figure out what you should do," Tori said. "I think you should spy on him and see if you can catch him with Cynthia."

"Do you really think so?" Jill asked. "Maybe I should just go over to his place tomorrow and talk to him."

Tori made a face. "That's no good."

"I think Jill's right," Haley declared. "The best thing to do is ask him about it right up front. After all, Jill, you want *him* to be honest with *you*, right?"

"Well, either way, there's something I have to tell you, Jill," Tori said. "Even if things do turn out okay with you and Ryan, I can't invite him to the wedding. See, my mom let me have only four invitations. I already gave three of them away, to Martina and Nikki and Dani. I haven't figured out what to do with the other one yet."

Haley's mouth dropped open. "You're kidding! The wedding is four days away."

Tori sighed. "But no matter what I do, I'm going to hurt someone's feelings. If I invite Ryan for Jill, then I should invite Alex for you, Haley. And if I invite Alex, I have to invite Patrick. Not to mention Amber, who thinks she's coming anyway! The whole thing's impossible. I wish my mom had given me a hundred invitations so that I could invite everyone I know."

"Well, don't worry. I'll understand if you can't invite Ryan," Jill said.

"Yeah, and you don't have to invite Alex for me, either," Haley told her.

"Thanks," Tori replied. "Though it's too bad the guys won't see you in your bridesmaids' dresses."

"Patrick said he'd come by my house before the wedding to take a picture," Haley said. She laughed at the idea.

"I can't wait to see our dresses," Jill said.

"Good, because we have to go straight to Zophia's for a fitting," Tori told her.

"All right!" Jill's eyes sparkled in excitement.

"And then I was hoping you'd help me shop," Tori added. "I still need to find a special present for my mom and Roger."

Jill glanced at her in surprise. "Really? Do you have to get your own mother something?"

"Tori *wants* to," Haley explained. "She's worried that Veronica will give them something incredible and make her look bad."

"It's not just that," Tori insisted. "My mom's given me so much in my life. She's always been there for me, and I know that's pretty hard, all on her own. And she really pushed me to be the best skater I can be, always paid for lessons and skating things and made me all those special skating dresses—I mean, she's just given me *everything*. Now this is my chance to give *her* something."

"That's really sweet, Tori," Jill said.

"Yeah, the only problem is, what can I get?" Tori shook her head. "We all searched the mall, but we couldn't find a thing."

"We found about a million things," Haley corrected. "But none of them was good enough."

"Well, it has to be extra special," Tori insisted.

Jill nodded. "You're right, Tori. I mean, the important stuff your mom has given you isn't the kind of thing you can find in a store."

"Yeah," Tori agreed.

A few minutes later the car pulled up in front of a two-story white building. It was an unusually warm day. It had snowed a few days earlier, and now the snow was melting. As they stepped out of the car Haley's foot landed in a big puddle.

"Watch out for the puddle," Haley told Jill and Tori. "That's why it's good that I always wear hiking boots," she said. "These can walk through anything."

"Those boots could *break* anything," Tori joked. She and Jill giggled. Then Tori pointed toward the building. "My mom said Zophia's shop is on the second floor."

Tori pulled open the door and started up the narrow steps. "I hope Veronica isn't here," she murmured.

Jill frowned. "Are you still worried that your mom might let Veronica be a maid of honor?" she asked.

"Yeah. I'm so worried, I couldn't even ask my mom whether or not it was true," Tori said.

At the top of the steps was a wooden door with a small sign that said ZOPHIA CZAIA, SEAMSTRESS. They hurried inside.

Zophia's face lit up when she saw them. "Ah, I have been waiting for you girls."

"This is my friend Jill," Tori said to Zophia. "And you remember Haley."

"Welcome, Jill." Zophia smiled. "You are as pretty as Tori and Haley."

Tori searched the small room. "Where's Veronica?"

"Oh, the young woman with the lovely figure? I finished with her," Zophia explained. "Your mother brought her in earlier. I had to make some changes in her dress."

"What kind of changes?" Tori asked.

Zophia shrugged. "Changes, that is all. Nothing to concern you, dear." She pointed to Haley. "I will take the redhead now. Here is your dress."

Zophia handed her a long maroon gown. Haley eyed the dress with interest. "I've never worn anything like that before in my life," Haley said.

"Don't worry, it won't bite you." Zophia laughed. "Change and come out when you are ready." Zophia pulled a curtain across a small alcove. Haley stepped inside. A minute later she pushed back the curtain. She was wearing the maroon dress.

"Haley, you look great!" Jill exclaimed.

Tori stared. "You look—so pretty," she said in surprise.

"Do I? Thanks!" Haley took a step forward.

"Watch out—your hiking boot," Tori began to say, but it was too late.

Haley tripped and pitched forward. "Yikes!" She waved her arms wildly, trying to catch her balance. There was a loud ripping sound as she sprawled onto the floor.

"The dress!" Tori and Zophia screamed at the same time.

"Haley, are you okay?" Jill called with concern.

Haley scrambled to her feet. "I heard something rip," she cried out. She turned around.

"Oh, no!" Tori felt sick to her stomach. The whole back of Haley's dress was ripped below the knees.

"It's *ruined!*" Tori cried out.

"Oh, Haley! You and your hiking boots," Jill exclaimed.

"I—I didn't mean to do it," Haley stammered. "They caught . . . I tripped." She swallowed hard.

Zophia bent over the dress. "I am afraid it cannot be repaired. The fabric is too badly torn."

"Are you sure?" Haley asked miserably.

"Well, if you can't fix it, you'll just have to make another one," Tori told her.

Zophia shook her head. "The fabric was specially ordered. I don't have any more of it. It's impossible to have another dress made in time for the wedding."

"What are we going to do?" Tori cried.

"I know one thing we can do," Haley said quietly. "I just won't be in the wedding, that's all." She paused. "The funny thing is, I was really looking forward to walking down the aisle."

"Haley, you have to be in the wedding," Tori protested. "We've been planning this for so long!"

"Then I won't be in the wedding," Jill suggested. "You can wear my dress, Haley."

Zophia shook her head. "I'm a good seamstress, but I can't make Jill's dress fit Haley's figure. Not perfectly. And it must be perfect!"

"She's right," Tori said. "Besides, Jill, you came all the way from Denver for this."

"I should be the one who drops out," Haley said. She twisted to gaze down at the ripped hem. "This wouldn't have happened if these were short dresses. I can't walk in a long dress," she complained.

"Well, you should have tried harder," Tori told her.

"Hey, wait a minute." Haley suddenly grinned. "What if we made my dress short?"

"But all the dresses have to match," Tori pointed out.

"So let's shorten them all," Haley said.

"That's ridiculous! This is a formal wedding," Tori began to argue.

"Bridesmaids can wear shorter dresses at a formal wedding," Zophia interrupted. "It's not a bad idea. I could lift the hem to just above the rip."

Tori's face brightened. "You think it would be all right?"

Zophia shrugged. "Why not?"

"I'll call my mom and see what she thinks." Tori grabbed the telephone and began to dial. "Zophia, if my mom says it's okay, can you do it in time?"

Zophia nodded. "I think so."

"Great!" Tori breathed a sigh of relief. "Haley, you're really a good friend. But I can't believe how many times you've almost ruined this wedding!" Tori exclaimed.

"It's true," Haley agreed. "First there was the close call with the Whitehall reservation, then the wrong date on Jill's invitation, and now this!"

"Well, I guess we've all learned one lesson," Tori said. "Putting together a big wedding is a lot harder than it looks!"

17. Jill

As the big day approaches, the excitement builds, and so does the pressure. Emotions run high. The members of the wedding must guard against arguments and confrontations. Remember, it's just nerves!

—The Complete Wedding Book

"No! No! No!" two-year-old Laurie Wong screamed.

Jill's father sighed. "Come now, Laurie, we have to put your snowsuit on."

"No snow-soup! No snow-soup!" Laurie cried, waving her little fists in the air. Jill smiled at the cute way Laurie talked.

"Let me try, Dad." Jill took the pink snowsuit from her father. Jill knew this snowsuit well. It had belonged to her sister Randi before it was Laurie's, and to Kristi before that. Unlike her little sisters and brothers, Jill never had to wear hand-me-downs. That was the best part of being the oldest.

"Laurie, do you know how to make snow soup?" Jill asked.

Laurie's eyes grew wide. She shook her head.

"It's a special recipe," Jill explained, slipping the

little girl's feet into the snowsuit. "You need just the right snow." Jill zipped up the snowsuit. "Okay, Dad, she's ready."

Mr. Wong grinned. "It sure is good to have you home, Jill." He called up the stairs. "Come on, Michael and Mark, let's go! Time to give Jill a ride to the rink!" Jill's five-year-old twin brothers scrambled down the stairs.

"My turn to sit in front!" Michael and Mark each called.

"Jill gets to sit in front today," Jill's father told them. Mr. Wong had taken time off from his job at the bank to spend a few more hours with Jill. Mrs. Wong had to work at the travel agency.

"That's okay, Dad. I'd really like to take a walk before practice," Jill said. Her stomach did a nervous flip-flop. She planned to walk over to the high school, which wasn't far from her house. Ryan would be getting out soon. It would probably be a good chance to talk to him.

"Really? Well, okay, honey," her father said. "I'll go pick up your brother and sisters from school, then. Have a good practice. I'll see you later."

"Thanks. Bye!" Jill called as she watched them leave. After they were gone, Jill quickly packed her skate bag and brushed out her hair. She checked herself in her bedroom mirror. She wanted to look her best for Ryan.

Jill reached the school a little early. She sat on a low stone wall across the street from the entrance.

The final bell rang. Kids poured out of the school. Jill's heart began to beat faster. She was feeling so many things at once. She was excited about seeing Ryan, but nervous about what they had to talk about.

Everything's probably fine, Jill assured herself. I'm probably imagining this whole problem.

Jill searched the crowd. Oh, no! she thought. I'm definitely not imagining *that*! There was Ryan—and he had his arm around another girl!

Jill couldn't believe it. The girl was tall, with shoulder-length dark blond hair. She turned and said something to Ryan, and the two of them laughed. Jill felt as if she was going to faint. She stood up. I have to get out of here, she told herself. She turned to run.

"Jill!" Ryan called after her. He had spotted her! He hurried toward her.

Jill ran faster. I don't want him to see me, she thought wildly. I don't want him to see how upset I am. Jill raced down Hartsdale Street in the direction of the rink.

When she arrived at the rink, she was panting heavily from the long run. She turned quickly to check behind her, but there was no one in sight. Ryan hadn't followed her. She wasn't sure if she was happy or disappointed.

Jill caught her breath, smoothed her hair, and pulled open the door. But the moment she set eyes on her old rink, a wave of emotion rushed over her. She burst out crying.

She heard Tori's voice behind her. "Jill, what is it? Are you okay? Why are you crying?"

"Oh, Tori, it's true! Ryan's going out with Cynthia!"

"Are you sure?" Tori asked.

Jill wiped at her eyes. "I saw them together just now. He had his arm around her." Jill couldn't stop the tears. She sobbed into Tori's shoulder. "It's because I went away, I know it. I wish I had never gone to Denver!"

Tori hugged her. "Jill, you don't mean that. Going to the Academy was the right decision. It's the best thing for your skating."

"But I've had to give up so much," Jill complained. "I'm *tired* of giving things up for my skating! You know it yourself, Tori. I almost couldn't come to the wedding because of skating."

Tori looked Jill in the eye. "Jill, you're a great skater, you know that. Your skating is more important than anything."

"Is it?" Jill asked.

Tori glanced down at the floor. "Yeah. And I'm sorry I pressured you so much about coming to the wedding. I know how important the senior-level test is." She glanced up at Jill and smiled a little. "In fact, if *I* had the chance to take that test, *I* might even miss the wedding!"

Jill laughed a little. "But why couldn't Ryan have been different? I thought I could count on him."

"Forget about Ryan," Tori told her. "He's not worth it. Go change, then get out on that ice and start working. You have only two days left before the test."

"You're right. Thanks, Tori." Jill headed into the locker room. But she couldn't stop crying. She was just so disappointed in Ryan. She didn't see how she would ever get over it.

The next two days passed in a blur of practicing and visiting with her old friends and family. Jill tried hard not to think about Ryan. But every day she still expected the phone to ring. She could hardly believe it when he didn't call.

Finally, on Friday, Jill was at the rink again, warming up for her test. It was just after lunch, and her friends from Silver Blades were all still in school. Jill was supposed to take the test with Kathy in half an hour.

She completed her warm-up and began to run through some of the moves she needed to pass the test. She worked on her footwork sequence, a series of choctaws, rockers, and spiral steps that she had to perform with clean edges and perfect form.

She finished the required steps, then decided to practice part of her new routine. She launched into a flying camel and then a back camel spin, allowing the rhythm of the skating to comfort her.

But as she prepared for a tuck axel and triple toe

loop, she suddenly thought of Ryan again. She completed only one and a half revolutions on the triple toe loop before touching down.

I'll have to do better than this, Jill thought as she continued to practice. How will it look if I flub my jumps and fail the test now? Especially after Ludmila took the trouble to arrange for me to take it here in Seneca Hills.

As Jill glided around the rink again she spotted a familiar figure standing at the boards. Ryan! Her stomach lurched.

"Hi, Jill," Ryan called.

Jill slowly skated over to him. She wondered if he would hug her or give her a kiss hello. But he remained standing with his hands at his sides.

Jill felt her throat tighten. "Hi, Ryan," she managed to say.

"Can you talk for a few minutes?" he asked.

"Well, actually, I'm pretty busy. I'm taking a test soon, the senior levels," Jill explained.

"Wow. That sounds important," Ryan said. "So it's probably not such a good time to bother you."

"I guess I could talk for a little while." Jill stepped off the ice. She wiped off her blades and slipped on her skate guards. She walked over to the bleachers and sat down. Ryan followed her.

For a moment neither one of them said a word. Finally Ryan sat next to her. Jill felt really uncomfortable.

"Jill, I'm sorry about the other day. I mean, when

you saw me with Cynthia like that," Ryan suddenly blurted.

Jill stared at him. Somehow she had still been hoping that it was all a big misunderstanding. For an instant she felt even worse than before. And then she felt a burst of anger.

"How could you do that to me? It was awful, seeing you two together like that," she told him.

"I know. I'm sorry," Ryan said. "I should have told you the truth."

Jill took a deep breath. "What *is* the truth, Ryan?"

"Well, Cynthia and I *were* just friends, in the beginning," Ryan told her. "But then things changed. I don't know, Jill. I mean, Cynthia's right here, and you're so far away."

"I know that!" Jill exploded. "Don't you think I feel the same way? But I didn't go sneaking around on you!"

Ryan stared at the floor. "I'm sorry."

"I'm sorry, too." Jill swallowed hard. "Maybe we shouldn't be together anymore. I mean, I guess we're *not* together," she said.

Ryan nodded. "I feel awful."

"Me too," Jill said. "But it's better this way."

"Yeah. I guess you might want to go out with some guy in Denver, anyway."

Jill thought of Jesse Barrow. "Maybe," she said.

They sat there awkwardly. Jill's stomach was tied up in knots. She was relieved when she spotted Kathy hurrying out of her office.

"There's my coach. I have to go now, Ryan, it's time for my test. You'd better go, too," Jill said.

"Okay." Ryan headed toward the exit. Jill slipped off her skate guards and stepped onto the ice again. Kathy walked over to her.

"Well, Jill, are you ready for the test?" her former coach asked.

Jill glanced toward the exit. Ryan had paused to watch her. He gave Jill a quick thumbs-up sign, then pushed through the doors.

Jill took a deep breath. Forget about Ryan, she told herself. For now, just think about skating.

"Yes, Kathy," Jill said. "I'm ready."

18. Tori

By the day before the wedding, everything is in place. This is a time when the bride appreciates extra attention from the groom, and from the maid of honor or bridesmaids—anyone who holds a unique place in her heart. She may have last-minute jitters that only a close friend, such as the maid of honor, would understand.

—The Complete Wedding Book

Tori rushed into the locker room. Haley, Martina, and Amber were right behind her. "Jill! Are you in here?" Tori called.

"Over here, Tori," Jill answered.

Tori hurried up to her. "Well, did you pass?" she demanded.

It was Friday afternoon, the day before the wedding. The members of Silver Blades were arriving for afternoon practice.

"I passed." Jill grinned. "The footwork went well, and my routine was perfect."

"That's fantastic!" Tori hugged Jill. She couldn't help feeling a twinge of jealousy, but she was also genuinely happy for her friend.

Haley dropped to her knees and bowed her head.

"Oh, genuine senior ladies' division skater, we salute you!"

Jill laughed out loud. "Thanks, Haley. But I'm just glad it's over."

"I'm really happy for you, Jill," Nikki said.

"Me too," Amber added.

"It's so exciting," Martina commented. "This means you can compete in Skate U.S.A., right?" she asked.

Jill groaned. "*Another* thing to start worrying about."

Everyone laughed.

"I wish I could pass the test," Amber mumbled. "How did you convince Ludmila that you were ready to take it?"

"I didn't, really," Jill admitted. "I just tried to skate my best, and then Ludmila decided I was ready."

Haley finished lacing up her skates. "Well, see you guys out on the ice."

"Haley!" Tori called after her. "Don't forget the dinner at my house tonight!"

"Dinner?" Amber looked interested.

Tori felt herself flush. "It's not very special," Tori explained. "It's just for the people in the wedding, the bridesmaids and everyone." She turned to Nikki and Martina. "Sorry you can't come either, guys."

"That's okay," Martina said.

"Sure," Nikki agreed. "Going to the wedding tomorrow is exciting enough for us."

"By the way, how did the dresses turn out, Tori?" Nikki asked. "Do they look good short?"

"I haven't seen them," Tori admitted. "But my mom loved the idea. She said they'd look much more fashionable that way." Tori raised her eyebrows. " 'Short formal dresses are all over the Paris fashion runways,' " she said, imitating Veronica.

"Did Veronica really say that?" Haley asked. "Then I guess it was a good thing I ripped my dress." She suddenly grinned. "Hey, who ever thought *I'd* be the expert on fashion?"

Later that evening Tori, Haley, and Jill sat at the Carsens' elegantly set dining room table. Tori's mother and Roger sat at either end. Roger's brother, George, and his wife, Midge, sat near him. Their six-year-old boy, Todd, sat next to Haley. Todd was going to be the ring bearer for the wedding ceremony.

Veronica was at the piano just on the other side of the arched doorway, playing a complicated classical piece.

"Can you believe the way she acts all dramatic? She always closes her eyes when she plays," Tori whispered to Jill. "She's such a fake."

"She sure can play well, though," Jill commented.

"Maybe closing her eyes helps her feel the music," Haley suggested.

Tori sighed. "Haley, that's ridiculous. *You* don't act like that when you play the piano."

"Tori, when I play the piano, I'm usually playing chopsticks," Haley pointed out.

Tori scooped up another bite of her fresh strawberries and let the spoon drop back into her bowl with a clatter. Her mother shot her a sharp glance of disapproval. Tori leaned back in her chair in frustration.

Finally the piece wound down to a close. Veronica sat still for a moment in silence. Then she opened her eyes.

"Bravo! Bravo!" Roger called. The guests applauded.

"That was spectacular," George said.

"A beautiful job, Veronica," Mrs. Carsen agreed.

Tori couldn't stand it anymore. "Hey, Mom," she said. "Did I tell you how well I did today with my triple toe loop? Dan said it was looking better than ever."

"That's wonderful, Tori," her mother said. She glanced around the table. "Can I get anyone anything? More coffee?"

"I'm just fine, thanks, Corinne," George said.

"You must have taken lessons for a long time, Veronica," Midge said as Veronica returned to the table.

"Veronica's a very serious musician," Roger said.

"Well, all the hard work you've put in certainly shows," Midge told her. "You've got a lot of talent."

"Why doesn't anyone ever talk about all the hard

work *I've* put into skating?" Tori complained to Jill in a whisper. "I wish I could make a skating rink appear in the middle of the dining room. I'd show everyone what talent is."

Mrs. Carsen cleared her throat. "I have a special announcement to make," Tori's mother said. She beamed at Veronica. "You don't mind if I tell everyone now, do you? Instead of saving the surprise for tomorrow?"

"Whatever you think is best, Corinne," Veronica said in her fake sweet voice.

Tori stared at her mother in alarm. Was she going to announce that she had made Veronica a maid of honor also?

"I've asked Veronica to have a special part in the wedding tomorrow," Mrs. Carsen went on.

Tori stared at Veronica, who returned Tori's look with a smug smile. Tori couldn't listen. "Excuse me," she announced. "I have to go to the bathroom."

"Tori, really," Mrs. Carsen said with an embarrassed laugh.

Tori felt everyone staring at her as she rushed out of the room. She hurried across the living room and ran up the stairs. How could her mother do this to her? Ever since Veronica had arrived, all she did was take everything away from Tori.

As Tori hurried past the guest room, the pale wood bureau in the corner caught her eye. The notebook! she thought. She dashed into the room and pulled open the top drawer of the dresser. She fished around until she felt the notebook.

"Yes!" Tori exclaimed. She pulled it out and opened it up. She searched through it eagerly. The check was still there, along with the page of signatures. And there were a few more pages where Veronica had practiced Adele's name. On a page near the back, Tori noticed a scrawl that read *Académie Martine.*

Then Tori noticed another piece of paper slipped into the very back. She slid it out. It was a letter.

ACADÉMIE MARTINE

26, RUE MARTINE

PARIS, FRANCE

Dear Mrs. Fouchard,

We regret to inform you that we will no longer be able to offer your daughter, Veronica, a place at our school. We feel that we have given Veronica every available opportunity to prove that she can succeed as a student at the Académie Martine, but she has been unable to do so.

Veronica is a very bright girl and a gifted musician. Unfortunately, it is also our conclusion that she is very troubled. She has been suspended three times this year for behavior problems and for breaking school rules. According to school policy, any student who is suspended three times must be expelled. We are sorry that Veronica was not able to create for herself at the Académie Martine the stable, secure environment she so desperately needs.

Please sign the enclosed form indicating that you have received this letter and return it to the school at your earliest convenience.

> *Sincerely,*
> *Mme. Marie Montaine*
> *School Director*

Tori gasped. So *this* was Veronica's secret! She had been kicked out of that fancy French school. No wonder Veronica had been practicing Adele's signature. Veronica planned to sign the letter herself and return it to the school. Veronica's mother probably didn't even know she'd been expelled!

Tori folded the letter and slipped it in her pocket. Just wait until she showed this to her mother and Roger! Veronica would be on the next plane back to France.

19. Tori

Even the best-planned weddings are sure to come up against unexpected difficulties. It is best to try to remain calm and think clearly should last-minute problems occur.

—The Complete Wedding Book

Tori bounded down the stairs. The letter from Académie Martine was safe inside her pocket. She couldn't wait to read it out loud.

"Mom, Roger, I have something really important to tell you," Tori began. "I—"

The phone rang.

"I'll get it, Corinne," Veronica volunteered.

Mrs. Carsen stood up. "No, that's all right, Veronica. I should have known we couldn't get through a meal without someone calling." She smiled as she left the room. "Well, at least it shouldn't have anything to do with the wedding. Thank goodness, everything's completely set for tomorrow."

Tori could hear her mother pick up the phone in the hall. Suddenly there was a loud shriek.

"What? That can't be! There must be a mistake!"

Mrs. Carsen's voice grew even louder. "No, no, you're not listening to me. I tell you, that's impossible!"

A moment later Mrs. Carsen rushed into the dining room. Her face was bright red, and she was shaking. "You simply will not believe this. That call was from the Whitehall Hotel. They wanted to know why the china and tableclothes were being delivered."

"They should let you set up those things the night before the wedding," Midge declared. "Shouldn't they, Corinne?"

"Yes, they should," Tori's mother said. "That's not the problem. The problem is that the Whitehall thinks the wedding is on *March* twenty-third. Not tomorrow, February twenty-third."

"What?" Roger exclaimed. "How did that happen? You made the reservation yourself, didn't you?"

Mrs. Carsen pressed a hand to her forehead. "I'm trying to think. That first time we went over, I spoke to someone . . . oh, what was her name?"

"Wasn't it Franny something?" Veronica asked.

"Franny Wyatt, that was it," Tori's mother said. "Didn't we speak to her again to confirm the date?"

"Uh, I did," Haley croaked.

Everyone turned to stare at her. Haley looked as if she wished she could sink into the floor.

"I talked to the woman from the Whitehall," Haley repeated.

"Haley, dear." Tori's mother had a strained look.

"Did she say anything about holding the reception in March?"

"No," Haley insisted. "I'm sure I would have noticed if she did."

"I don't get it. What does this mean?" Tori demanded.

"It means we have nowhere to hold the wedding reception tomorrow." Mrs. Carsen collapsed into her chair.

"It's my fault," Haley said. "I can't believe I messed up again! First Jill's invitation, then the dresses—now this!"

"But why did *you* talk to the Whitehall?" Tori asked her friend.

"Your mom asked me to, remember? It was that day when all those people were here and everyone was rushing around," Haley explained. "The Whitehall called and said they were checking the reservation for the twenty-third. I figured they meant *February* twenty-third. So I said okay."

"But it turns out they meant *March* twenty-third," Jill pointed out.

"Well, I didn't know that. And they did have the time wrong," Haley added. "I corrected them about that."

"Well, it's clearly the Whitehall's fault," Mrs. Carsen said briskly. "The question is, what are we going to do about it?"

"I guess we're just going to have to wait for March," Roger said.

"What? That's impossible, Roger," Mrs. Carsen snapped. "Everything is arranged for tomorrow—the food, the music, the flowers. Many of the guests have arrived from out of town. We can't possibly put it off."

"What about having it here?" Veronica suggested.

"No way," Tori said. "This house is big, but it can't fit two hundred and fifty people."

"Tori's right," Mrs. Carsen said. "We'll have to think of someplace else."

Haley's face lit up. "I have an idea." Then she looked embarrassed. "I mean, you might not like it, but it's definitely a big place."

"Where?" Roger asked.

"The rink," Haley said. "It can fit two hundred and fifty people."

For a moment everyone was silent.

"That's a great idea!" Tori cried. "We can have the reception on ice!"

"That's ridiculous," Veronica scoffed. "What about the people who can't skate?"

"Well, there's plenty of room off the ice, too," Haley pointed out.

"She's right. Why not have it there?" Roger asked.

They all turned to Mrs. Carsen. A smile spread across her face. "Yes. Yes, I think I like it," she pronounced. "It's unique. There's plenty of room for the tables and the band. Oh, and won't all those pink flowers look lovely beside the white ice!"

"A wedding on ice! With the bride and groom skating their first dance! It sounds really pretty," Midge agreed.

"It's silly," Veronica said. She strolled over to the piano and began to tinkle lightly with the keys.

"Well, I think it's great!" Tori exclaimed, beaming. "Hey, Mom, if we're going to have the reception at the rink, can I invite a few more of my friends?"

Her mother looked at her. "Tori, I gave you your four invitations."

"But, Mom," Tori pleaded, "I can't invite just *some* of my friends. Not if it's going to be a skating party."

Mrs. Carsen hesitated. Suddenly she threw up her hands. "Why not? Go ahead. Everything else has changed. And after all, it *is* a celebration."

"Oh, Mom, thanks!" Tori said. "I'll call everyone right now."

"First let me call Mrs. Bowen, the president of Silver Blades. I want to make sure we can arrange it." Tori's mother stood up. "There is just one thing I'm worried about, though."

"What's that, sweetheart?" Roger asked.

"You." She pointed a finger at him. "Poor Roger can't skate to save his life," she told everyone. "Who's going to hold my groom up when we dance on ice?"

They all laughed. Roger laughed with them. "I guess I'll just have to do my best," he said with a mysterious smile.

An hour later everything was settled. Mrs. Carsen had reserved the rink for the reception and made sure that the food and the flowers would be delivered there. She had also called the bandleader and instructed him to tell all the musicians about the change of location.

Tori said good-bye to her friends. George and Midge took Todd back to their hotel to put him to bed. Tori, her mother, and Roger drifted into the living room. Veronica still sat at the piano, playing quietly. Suddenly Tori remembered the letter. With all the fuss about the reception, she had completely forgotten it!

She pulled it out of her pocket. "Hey, listen—"

Veronica stood up. "I think I'll go upstairs to my room."

Tori flinched. She hated the way Veronica called the guest room *her* room. Veronica really thought she could take over the house. But Tori would put a stop to that—right away.

"Wait, Veronica. I think you might want to stick around and listen to this." Tori waved the piece of paper in her hand.

Veronica turned around. "Tori, I'm too tired to play games now, okay? I really want to get to bed and rest up for the wedding tomorrow."

"Tori, what is that in your hand?" Mrs. Carsen asked.

"A letter," Tori said, still waving the paper. "From the Académie Martine."

Veronica's face turned white. "Where did you get that?"

Tori smiled. "Where do you think?"

Veronica lunged at Tori and tried to grab the letter. "That's mine. Give it back to me!"

"Not before I show it to my mother," Tori replied, stuffing the letter between two couch cushions.

"Girls," Roger Arnold said sternly. "What's going on here?"

"Tori! Veronica! Stop that this instant!" Tori's mother exclaimed.

"Mom, listen! Veronica was kicked out of school," Tori said in a rush. "She was suspended three times, and now she can't go back."

Mrs. Carsen and Roger exchanged glances. Veronica stared down at the floor.

Tori blinked in surprise. Why wasn't anyone yelling at Veronica?

"Didn't you hear me?" Tori said. "Veronica got kicked out. It's all in this letter. Her mother's supposed to sign it and send it back to the school. But she doesn't even know that Veronica got expelled."

Roger cleared his throat. "She knows."

"What?" Tori and Veronica said together.

"But I took the letter out of the mailbox when I was home at Christmas," Veronica blurted out.

"Yes, but the school spoke with your mother on the phone," Mrs. Carsen told her.

"Wait a minute, Mom," Tori said in astonishment. "You *knew* about this already?"

"We've been in touch with Adele," Roger replied. "You're in some serious trouble, Veronica."

At last! Tori thought with relief. Now she's in for it.

"I knew it! I should have made that phone call to France sooner," Veronica muttered. "If I had called the school sooner, I could have kept them from calling my mother."

"So *that's* what you were doing that morning we caught you on the phone!" Tori exclaimed.

"Yes. I wanted to reach the school office while it was morning in France," Veronica admitted.

"I knew she was lying, Mom!" Tori crowed in triumph.

"Tori, please," said her mother. She turned to Veronica. "Roger and I have been discussing this, and I have something to say. But first I want to tell you that I don't appreciate being lied to, Veronica."

Veronica hung her head. Tori gazed around happily. Finally Veronica was going to get the punishment she deserved.

"Corinne's right, Veronica," Roger agreed. "If this is going to work out, you're going to have to learn to be honest with us from now on."

"If *what's* going to work out?" Tori demanded. She felt uneasy.

"Tori, this goes for you, too," her mother said. "We're all going to have to try to learn to get along here and respect one another."

"Why? What are you talking about?" Tori asked.

Roger cleared his throat. "Corinne and I have decided, and Adele agrees, that . . ." He looked at Mrs. Carsen.

"Veronica," Tori's mother said, "we'd like you to stay with us for a while. This can be your new home."

Tori's mouth dropped open. She stared at her mother in shock and disbelief. *This* was Veronica's punishment?

20. Tori

After all the plans and preparations, nothing can compare with the satisfaction provided by a major celebration that has been organized to perfection, so that all can enjoy the wedding itself.
                    —The Complete Wedding Book

Tori waited in the wedding chapel, smoothing the skirt of her gorgeous pink dress. She gazed with pleasure around the beautiful chapel with its colorful stained-glass windows. She couldn't believe it was finally the day of the wedding. The ceremony was due to start soon.

The door to the chapel opened, and Jill, Nikki, and Martina rushed in.

"Hi, Tori," Nikki said. Her green eyes were sparkling. "I hope you don't mind that we came with Jill."

"No! I told Jill it would be fun." Tori hugged all her friends.

Jill slipped out of her coat. She looked beautiful in the maroon bridesmaid's dress. And the new shorter length was perfect. "Is Haley here yet?"

"Not yet. Veronica is waiting in the back," Tori informed her. "She's giving Roger's sister-in-law a lecture on what kinds of hats are fashionable in Paris this year."

Jill laughed. "I guess it's going to be pretty hard for Veronica to get used to living in boring old Seneca Hills."

"Not as hard as it's going to be for us to get used to having her here," Tori complained. "I can't believe my mom and Roger actually invited her to move in."

Martina smiled. "You seem to be taking it pretty well, though, Tori."

Tori shrugged. "I guess I'm too relieved to think about it right now."

"Relieved about what?" Nikki asked.

"That Veronica's special part in the wedding didn't turn out to be that of the maid of honor," Jill said.

Tori giggled. "Actually I think it's great. My mom invited her to play a special piece on the organ during the ceremony," she explained to Nikki and Martina.

The two girls stared at her. "And you're glad?" Nikki asked.

Tori nodded. "Know where the organ is?" She pointed up to a balcony overlooking the chapel.

Martina squinted. "I don't see anything."

"That's the whole point," Tori said. "You can't see the organ, which means no one will be able to see Veronica. She'll walk down the aisle as a bridesmaid, but then she has to go up some secret staircase to get to the organ. She won't even stand up front with the rest of us during the ceremony."

Nikki laughed. "Tori, are you sure this wasn't your idea?"

The door to the chapel opened. "Hey, Haley," Martina said.

Tori swiveled. She was dying to see what Haley looked like in her dress. But when she saw her friend, she gaped. Haley was wearing her maroon bridesmaid's dress under her parka, which was open in front. But the dress had been shortened to the barest mini Tori had ever seen!

"Haley, what did you do?" Tori groaned.

"How could you?" Jill exclaimed. "It's *too* short!"

Haley slipped out of her jacket and spun around like a model. "Doesn't it look great? I came up with the idea this morning. I figured that since I'm the fashion expert now, I couldn't go wrong. Besides, I hear they're wearing micro-minidresses on the fashion runways in Paris."

"But Haley, it looks awful!" Tori declared.

"And it doesn't match Jill's," Nikki pointed out.

"Gotcha!" Haley cried with a huge grin. "Don't worry, Tori, I didn't really shorten it. It's just taped. It'll come out in a second. But you should have seen the look on your face!"

Tori breathed a sigh of relief—and punched Haley in the arm. "Why did I ever let you be a bridesmaid?" Then she burst out laughing. After all her worries about the wedding, it felt great to be laughing with her friends again.

The ceremony was beautiful. Tori felt so proud marching down the aisle and standing next to her mother and her friends in the chapel. Tori thought her mom looked beautiful in her petal pink gown. And Tori felt like a princess in her own dress.

Later, when the ceremony was over, Tori stood beside her mother and Roger again. The rest of the wedding party lined up behind them inside the entrance to the Ice Arena. It was time for the receiving line. The bride and groom and the wedding party waited to greet their guests and accept congratulations. Tori heard murmurs of appreciation as people arrived and gazed around.

The arena was almost unrecognizable. The dimmed lights shone softly on the lavish bouquets of pink flowers that lined the windows and the rink. The band was set up by the bleachers, playing soft music. Several tables piled high with refreshments stood near the offices. The tables were arranged to one side of the figure-skating rink, where a small space was also cleared for dancing. Two special tables were lined with pairs of ice skates, polished and ready for the guests to wear. The ice gleamed under the soft pastel-colored lights.

Kathy and Dan were among the first to arrive. Tori noticed that Dan gave Roger an extra-warm clap on the back as they shook hands. Tori was surprised. Roger and Dan barely knew each other.

"Mrs. Arnold!" A tall, dark-haired woman with a camera pushed through the crowd. Tori jumped with surprise. It sounded funny to hear her mom called "Mrs. Arnold." Tori's mother had explained that she was keeping the Carsen name for business but that many people would call her by Roger's last name.

"Mrs. Arnold, I'm from the *Seneca Star*," the woman explained. "Could I get a picture, please?"

"Sure," Tori answered. "I'm the daughter," she said.

"Oh, wonderful," the woman said. "Just stand next to the bride. And maybe I could have all the bridesmaids in the back."

Jill, Haley, and Veronica filed behind Tori's mother and Roger. Tori was disappointed that Veronica was going to be in the picture. But at least she's in the back, Tori told herself.

The woman snapped a few pictures and smiled. "Thanks a lot, everyone."

"You should stay for the rest of the reception," Tori suggested. "Everyone's going to put on skates and get out on the ice."

"That might be a great picture. I think I will," the woman told her.

"Nice work, Tori," her mother whispered. "Maybe the *Star* will do a whole story on the wedding. That would be excellent publicity." Mrs. Carsen threw an arm around Tori's shoulders and gave her a squeeze. "I'm so proud of you, Tori," she whispered into her ear.

Tori gazed up at her mother. "You are?"

"Of course," her mother responded. "I know these past few weeks haven't been easy for you."

Tori smiled at her mother gratefully. "I *have* been feeling kind of left out," she admitted.

Mrs. Carsen's eyes fixed on her daughter's. "Tori, I know there have been a lot of changes lately. And there will be a lot more as we get used to living together. But one thing will never change, and that's my love for you."

Tori threw her arms around her mother. "I love you, too, Mom."

Roger beamed at them. "Excuse me, Corinne, but Ken Slater's over there. He's one of my biggest customers. We should really go say hello."

Tori watched as her mother and Roger slipped through the crowd.

Haley came up behind Tori. "This is kind of fun," she said.

Tori smiled at her. "You mean maybe you'll start wearing dresses once in a while?"

"No way," Haley said. "It's the party that's fun, not the dress." She wriggled uncomfortably. "I don't know how I'm ever going to skate in this thing."

"Speaking of which, let's go put on our skates," Jill suggested.

"Good idea," Nikki agreed. The girls headed to the locker room and changed into their skates. They hurried back out to the rink, and Nikki pointed toward the ice. "Look—Martina, Amber, and Patrick are already out there."

The band was playing lively music, and the ice was starting to fill up with skaters. It was easy to pick out the Silver Blades skaters from the rest of the crowd. Some of the guests were hanging on to the railing at the edge of the ice.

Haley laughed. "We could make a bundle giving lessons today, right, Tori?"

Tori didn't answer. She was staring at the ice. "That looks like Roger," she muttered. "But it couldn't be. He can't skate at all. And this guy is skating pretty smoothly." Tori squinted. "It's definitely Roger!"

Roger glided over to her. "How am I doing?" He grinned.

"Not bad!" Tori exclaimed. "How did *you* learn to skate?"

"Same way you did, Tori," said Roger with a grin. "Lessons."

"Lessons?" Tori was amazed. "But with who? When?"

Roger laughed. "With your coach, Dan. Kathy arranged for me to have a few lessons with him when we knew you and your mom wouldn't be here. I wanted to learn to skate, even before we decided to have the reception here. I know how important skating is to you and your mom, and I wanted us to skate together as a family."

"Wow, that's really sweet," Tori told him.

"I'd better go out there and catch up with Corinne," Roger said. "I hope we can skate together later, Tori."

Tori watched as Roger skated off.

"If he really wants to skate as a family, he'd better get Veronica lessons fast," Haley said. She nodded toward the ice. Veronica was clutching the railing with a terrified look on her face.

Jill, Nikki, Haley, and Tori burst out laughing. "I guess Veronica isn't an expert on *everything*," Tori said.

"Yeah. But wasn't that nice of Roger, to take secret skating lessons?" Jill asked. "He must really care about your mom. That's a special present."

"Hey! You just gave me a great idea, Jill!" Tori grabbed her and hugged her hard.

"What?" Jill asked, confused. "What did I say?"

"The wedding present! Something special for my mom and Roger," Tori explained. "Something that can't be bought in a store. Well, how about a skating show, just for them?"

"Here?" Jill asked. "Now?"

"Why not?" Tori replied. "We could all change into practice clothes and do our routines."

"What about the music?" Jill asked. "We can't expect the band to know our songs."

"I've got my tape in my locker," Haley volunteered. "We could play it on the sound system."

"I think I've got mine in my bag," Jill said.

"Our tapes are in the locker room," Nikki said, nodding at Martina. "Let's do it!"

"Oh, no," Tori cried. "My tape of 'Forever' is at home!"

"You could skate without music," Haley suggested.

"That's no good," Tori complained. "It'll look dumb if I'm the only one without music. Besides, 'Forever' is such a romantic song. It's perfect for a wedding ice show."

"I know!" Haley said. "Veronica could play 'Forever' on the piano."

"She *does* know the song," Tori said. "She drove me crazy one night playing this really show-offy version. I guess it would actually work for my routine."

Tori headed reluctantly to the railing, where Veronica was trying to stay upright.

"Hi, Veronica," Tori said. Veronica nearly jumped in surprise. "Boy, you sure are tense out on the ice," Tori remarked.

"So?" Veronica let go of the railing and nearly fell. She grabbed the railing again. Tori had to laugh. "What's so funny?" Veronica demanded.

"Nothing," Tori said, hiding a smile. "Listen, I want to ask you a big favor. Do you remember the song 'Forever'? The song I use for my new routine?"

"I remember every piece I play," Veronica answered.

"Do you think you could play it again?" Tori asked. "Here, on the band's keyboard?"

"I suppose. Why?" Veronica asked.

Tori hesitated. "Well, actually, it's going to be my wedding present for Mom and Roger," she explained.

Veronica shrugged. "Sure, I'll play it for you, I guess. But you have to do me a favor in return."

"What's that?" Tori asked with suspicion.

Veronica gave her a pleading look. "Get me off this ice before I break my neck!"

Tori laughed. "Sure, no problem." She held out her hand, and Veronica grabbed it. Together they left the ice.

Fifteen minutes later everything was ready. The guests were assembled on the bleachers, with Tori's mother and Roger in the front row. The bandleader called for attention.

"And now, a very special gift for the bride and groom from the bride's daughter, Tori, with some help from her friends. Presenting . . . an ice-skating tribute to the happy couple!"

The crowd broke into applause. Tori felt a nervous twitch in her stomach. Although she had skated in front of large groups many times before, this time was special. This was for her mother.

Jill performed first. As the notes of "Yes, I Can" floated over the glistening ice, Jill glided elegantly into the opening moves of her routine. It was the first time Tori had seen Jill perform the new program to music. Tori was impressed—not only with Jill's technique, but with the emotion she poured into her skating.

Tori frowned. Jill seemed to know what Dan meant when he told Tori to "feel the music."

Jill launched into her final sit spin, and Tori felt a burst of pride. The guests broke into enthusiastic applause. Tori glanced at her mom and Roger. They were really enjoying the show.

Next Haley and Patrick took their places on the ice. The upbeat notes of 'We're a Team' began, and Haley and Patrick skated and clowned through their opening moves. When they imitated each other's moves, everyone in the bleachers laughed and clapped along. The routine ended with Patrick lifting Haley into a dynamic star-lift followed by a death spiral that left the audience standing on its feet. Tori was thrilled. The show was spectacular.

Nikki and Alex came next and wowed the crowd with their program. Then Martina performed a lovely number that showed off her dramatic style. Finally it was Tori's turn.

Tori watched as Veronica sat down at the keyboard. Tori took a deep breath. She really wanted her performance to be special. She wanted to be perfect for her mother and Roger.

Tori skated onto the ice and took her position. The crowd fell completely silent. Tori nodded to Veronica, and the first notes of 'Forever' echoed throughout the rink. Tori pushed off into the opening of her routine.

She circled the rink in a series of spread-eagles,

her entire body tilting back like a sail in the wind. The romantic music swept her along. Veronica played beautifully, and Tori let herself skate more freely than she had ever skated before.

She lifted easily into her double Lutz—double loop combination and landed without even noticing. Before she knew it, she had completed a triple toe loop and finished the middle portion of her program.

Her final jumps, a triple salchow and double flip, seemed easier than ever before. I'm doing it, Tori realized with a start. I'm *feeling* the music! A chill wound down her spine. I know what Dan means, she thought. There really *is* a difference!

With a burst of excitement she launched into the end of the routine, finishing with a graceful layback spin, changing arm positions dramatically. As the crowd burst into wild applause, Tori held her final pose.

She had never skated as well in her life, and she knew the reason why. This routine was a gift—a gift to her mother. Tori flung her arms above her head and smiled until her cheeks ached. The crowd kept on applauding.

Tori opened her eyes to see that everyone in the audience had leaped to their feet. Her mother and Roger climbed quickly down from their seats and hurried to meet Tori at the boards. They hugged Tori and kissed her proudly. Even Veronica applauded.

Tori had another sudden realization: This was her family now. The day before, it had been just Tori and her mom—the Carsen team. But that night the four of them—Tori, her mom, Roger, and Veronica—would be going home to the same house.

She had no idea what her new family life would be like. With Veronica around, it certainly wasn't going to be dull!

Tori shook her head in amazement. When she was a little girl, she used to feel jealous of other kids. Sometimes she had wished for a big family. But never in her wildest dreams had she imagined that she would get one this way!

But then, she reminded herself, nothing that had happened in the past few weeks had been what she'd expected. No doubt about it, Tori thought as she beamed at the crowd—life is full of surprises!

#5: The Perfect Pair

Nikki Simon and Alex Beekman are the perfect pair on the ice. But off the ice there's a big problem. Suddenly Alex is sending Nikki gifts and asking her out on dates. Nikki wants to be Alex's partner in pairs but not his girlfriend. Will she lose Alex when she tells him? Can Nikki's friends in Silver Blades find a way to save her friendship with Alex *and* her skating career?

#6: Skating Camp

Summer's here and Jill can't wait to join her best friends from Silver Blades at skating camp. It's going to be just like old times. But things have changed since Jill left Silver Blades to train at a famous ice academy. Tori and Danielle are spending all their time with another skater, Haley Arthur, and Nikki has a big secret that she won't share with anyone. Has Jill lost her best friends forever?

#7: The Ice Princess

Tori's favorite skating superstar, Elyse Taylor, is in town, and she's staying with Tori! When Elyse promises to teach Tori her famous spin, Tori's sure they'll become the best of friends. But Elyse isn't the sweet champion everyone thinks she is. And she's going to make problems for Tori!

#8: Rumors at the Rink

Haley can't believe it—Kathy Bart, her favorite coach in the whole world, is quitting Silver Blades! Haley's sure it's all her fault. Why didn't she listen when everyone told her to stop playing practical jokes on Kathy? With Kathy gone, Haley knows she'll never win the next big competition. She has to make Kathy change her mind—no matter what. But will Haley's secret plan work?

#9: Spring Break

Jill is home from the Ice Academy, and everyone is treating her like a star. And she loves it! It's like a dream come true—especially when she meets cute, fifteen-year-old Ryan McKensey. He's so fun and cool—and he happens to be her number-one fan! The only problem is that he doesn't understand what it takes to be a professional athlete. Jill doesn't want to ruin her chances with such a great guy. But will dating Ryan destroy her future as an Olympic skater?

#10: Center Ice

It's gold medal time for Tori—she just knows it! The next big competition is coming up, and Tori has a winning routine. Now all she needs is that fabulous skating dress her mother promised her! But Mrs. Carsen doesn't seem to be interested in Tori's skating anymore—not since she started dating a new man in town. When Mrs. Carsen tells Tori she's not going to the competition, Tori decides enough is enough! She has a plan that will change everything—forever!

#11: A Surprise Twist

Danielle's on top of the world! All her hard work at the rink has paid off. She's good. Very good. And Dani's new English teacher, Ms. Howard, says she has a real flair for writing—she might even be the best writer in her class. Trouble is, there's a big skating competition coming up—*and* a writing contest. Dani's stumped. Her friends and family are counting on her to skate her best. But Ms. Howard is counting on her to write a winning story. How can Dani choose between skating and her new passion?

#12: The Winning Spirit

A group of Special Olympics skaters is on the way to Seneca Hills! The skaters are going to pair up with the Silver Blades members in a mini-competition. Everyone in Silver Blades thinks Nikki Simon is really lucky—her Special Olympics partner is Carrie, a girl with Down syndrome who's one of the best visiting skaters. But Nikki can't seem to warm up to the idea of skating with Carrie. In fact, she seems to be hiding something . . . but what?

#13: The Big Audition

Holiday excitement is in the air! Jill Wong, one of Silver Blades' best skaters, is certain she will win the leading role of Clara in the *Nutcracker on Ice* spectacular. Until young skater Amber Armstrong comes along. At first Jill can't believe that Amber is serious competition. But she had better believe it—and fast! Because she's about to find herself completely out of the spotlight.

#14: Nutcracker on Ice

Nothing is going Jill Wong's way. She hates her role in the *Nutcracker on Ice* spectacular. And she's hardly on the ice long enough to be noticed! To top it all off, the Ice Academy coaches seem awfully impressed with Jill's main rival, Amber Armstrong. Jill has worked so hard to return to the Academy, and now she might lose her chance. Does Jill have what it takes to save her lifelong dream?

Super Edition #1: Rinkside Romance

Tori, Haley, Nikki, and Amber are at the Junior Nationals, where a figure skater's dreams can really come true! But Amber's trying too hard, and her skating is awful. Tori's in trouble with an important judge. Nikki and Alex are fighting so much they might not make it into the competition. And someone is sending them all mysterious love notes! Are their skating dreams about into turn into nightmares?

#15: A New Move

Haley's got a big problem. Lately her parents have been fighting more than ever. And now her dad is moving out—and going to live in Canada! Haley just doesn't see how she can live without him. Especially since the only thing her mom and sister ever talk about is her sister's riding. They don't care about Haley's skating at all! There's one clever move that could solve all Haley's problems. Does she have the nerve to go through with it?

#16: Ice Magic

Martina Nemo has always dreamed of skating in the Ice Capades. So when she lands a skating role in a television movie, it seems too good to be true! Martina loves to perform in front of the camera. It's a lot of fun—especially when all her friends in Silver Blades visit her on the set to cheer her on. Then Martina discovers something terrible: Someone is out to ruin her chance of a lifetime. . . .

#17: A Leap Ahead

Amber Armstrong is only eleven, but she can already skate as well as—even better than—the older girls in Silver Blades. The only problem is that the other skaters still treat her like a baby. So Amber decides to take the senior-level skating test. She'll be the youngest skater ever to pass, and then the other girls will *have* to stop treating her like a little kid. Amber is sure her plan will work. But is she headed for success or for total disaster?

#18: More Than Friends

Nikki's furious. Her skating partner, Alex, and her good friend, Haley, are dating each other. Nikki knows she shouldn't be jealous, but she is. She'd do anything to break them up. And she knows how to do it, too. But should she? Or will Nikki end up with no friends at all?

LEARN TO SKATE!

SKATE WITH U.S.
A SPECIAL PROGRAM FOR BEGINNERS

WHAT IS **SKATE WITH U.S.?**

Designed by the United States Figure Skating Association (USFSA) and sponsored by the United States Postal Service, Skate With U.S. is a beginning ice-skating program that is fun, challenging, and rewarding. Skaters of all ages are welcome!

HOW DO I JOIN **SKATE WITH U.S.?**

Skate With U.S. is offered at many rinks and clubs across the country. Contact your local rink or club to see if it offers the USFSA Basic Skills program. Or **call 1-800-269-0166** for more information about the Skate With U.S. program in your area.

WHAT DO I GET WHEN I JOIN **SKATE WITH U.S.?**

When you join Skate With U.S. through a club or a rink, you will be registered as an official USFSA Basic Skills Member, and you will receive:

- Official Basic Skills Membership Card
- Basic Skills Record Book with stickers
- Official Basic Skills member patch
- Year patch, denoting membership year
  And much, much more!

PLUS you may be eligible to participate in a "Compete With U.S." competition hosted by sponsoring clubs and rinks!

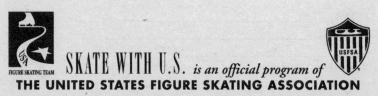

SKATE WITH U.S. *is an official program of*
THE UNITED STATES FIGURE SKATING ASSOCIATION

A FAN CLUB—JUST FOR YOU!

JOIN THE USA FIGURE SKATING INSIDE TICKET FAN CLUB!

As a member of this special skating fan club, you get:

- **Six issues of SKATING MAGAZINE!**
  For the inside edge on what's happening on and off the ice!

- **Your very own copy of MAGIC MEMORIES ON ICE!**
  A 90-minute video produced by ABC Sports featuring the world's greatest skaters!

- **An Official USA FIGURE SKATING TEAM Pin!**
  Available only to Inside Ticket Fan Club members!

- **A limited-edition photo of the U.S. World Figure Skating Team!**
  Available only to Inside Ticket Fan Club members!

- **The Official USA FIGURE SKATING INSIDE TICKET Membership Card!** For special discounts on USA Figure Skating collectibles and memorabilia!

To join the USA FIGURE SKATING INSIDE TICKET Fan Club, fill out the form below and send it with $24.95, plus $3.95 for shipping and handling (U.S. funds only, please!), to:

> Sports Fan Network
> USA Figure Skating Inside Ticket
> P.O. Box 581
> Portland, Oregon 97207-0581

Or call the Sports Fan Network membership hotline at **1-800-363-8796!**

NAME:_____

ADDRESS:_____

CITY:_____ **STATE:**_____ **ZIP:**_____

PHONE: (____)_____**DATE OF BIRTH:**_____